The Minister's Maid

Jamie DeBree

The Minister's Maid
ISBN 9781937477691
The Minister's Maid Copyright © 2012 Jamie M DeBree
Published by Brazen Snake Books
All rights reserved.

Edited by Carol R. Ward

Also by the Author

Tempest

Desert Heat

The Minister's Maid

Indelibly Inked

Heart Knocks

Chapter One

Betsy Majors slid the tray of empty champagne flutes onto the counter, adjusted the white lace collar over her chest and then reached for a fresh round of drinks. *Deep breath in, deep breath out, and smile*, she coached herself before backing through the swinging door into the lavish dining room. Silverware clattered against white stoneware plates over the low rumble of voices, ringing in her ears as she made her way to the other end of the table. She leaned over to replace empty glasses with full, keenly aware of eyes glued to her cleavage and fingers grazing her ass and thighs as she worked. It came with the French maid costume, and in the two years she'd been playing the part she'd learned that constant motion was the best offense.

"Another drink, monsieur?" she purred in her best French accent, placing a flute in front of an older gentleman to her right. He smiled shyly and nodded as she moved to the right. The group was part of a business conference currently taking place in Reno that had booked the Millionaire Mansion for a fun and exotic night out for its VIP crowd. So far everyone had been on good behavior, but that was to be expected. The rules of conduct for the Fantasy Ranch were strict and laid out when each booking was made, then again when each individual arrived. No violence, sex only between consenting adults and no abuse of the staff were the top three, and every fantasy scene included several burly security guards to make sure everyone complied. Betsy and Harley had wanted the ranch to be a safe place for people to explore their fantasies.

She glanced through the open double doors into the hall at the stately grandfather clock. Eleven o' clock. The party would be shifting into the parlor soon for brandy and cigars, and she'd start cleaning up while the other girls served after-dinner drinks. Tucking her now-empty tray under her arm, she started back toward the kitchen just as the man at the head of the table clinked his knife against a crystal glass.

"I'd like to thank you all for coming tonight," he said as the rumble died down to a low murmur. "It's been a great conference, and your support is what keeps our company running." There was a smattering of applause in return before he held his hands up to quiet the crowd. "I've been informed that we have brandy and cigars in the parlor if you'd like to join me down the hall." The guests clapped again, chairs scraping back against the tile floor as everyone rose almost at once. Betsy stood still against the wall just to the side of an ornate marble buffet table. She knew from experience that it was safer to stay put when such a large crowd was transitioning from one room to another. A smile pasted on her face, she idly watched the faces go by.

Then one caught her eye from across the room and she froze, feeling the blood drain from her face as she watched him walk past on the other side of the table. "No," she whispered, her pulse pounding as she fought the urge to run. "It can't be..."

As soon as the man went through the doors she pushed through the crowd to the kitchen, stopping only long enough to set her tray on the counter and tell one of the other girls she had to leave. Then she sprinted out the back door and through the alley, cautious to avoid the main road as she ran toward the chapel at the back of the compound.

* * *

Ian Mitchell frowned at the screen, deleting the paragraph he'd just written. There wasn't any good way to write a resignation letter and this was particularly difficult because he and Harley had been friends for so long. But he couldn't stay. Not with Betsy here, taunting him mercilessly with his own desire. He'd thought after being away from her for the past three years that he had a handle on his feelings, but it was increasingly clear that he'd never get over the crush that had started when they were just kids. It would be different if she wanted him for more than just a fling, but Betsy wasn't the type to settle down, and he wasn't sure he could survive letting her go after she tired of him. The thought that maybe she'd decide to stay with him sent his mother's voice whispering through his mind.

You should never try to change people, Ian. Accept them as they are. Then you won't be disappointed.

A noise from the hall drew his attention and he sighed. He'd been hoping for a quiet night to get this letter done and take it to Harley, but the only people who normally looked for him after hours were people wanting to get married on a whim. He hated doing impulse weddings - it was one of the other reasons he was leaving the ranch. In his experience people who decided to get married on a whim generally gave it no more thought than buying a cup of coffee. He wondered how many of the people he'd married in the year he'd been on the ranch were still together.

Someone knocked three times on his door and he stood, steeling himself for the inevitable and pasting a calm smile on his face. "Come in."

The door opened slowly and his pulse sped up as a familiar pixie face appeared in the opening. The object of his fantasies stepped into the room as if he'd conjured her straight from his dreams. Long blond hair swung in a high pony tail, accentuating a long, slender neck and snow white skin. She'd never been able to hold a tan in all the years he'd known her. She must have come straight from the mansion, and his cock stirred as he took in the slight French maid's costume that constituted her uniform. Between the crest of cleavage threatening to spill over the low scoop neck and the black garters flirting just under her hemline, no man alive had a chance of resisting her charms.

"Betsy - come in." His voice came out scratchy and raw and he cleared his throat, heat rising in his cheeks. "What can I do for you?"

She grinned, the worried look on her face relaxing at his words. "You know the answer to that, Ian," she said, sauntering forward with a hip-swing designed to drive men wild. He shook his head, brushing off her seductive moves. She'd always been a flirt.

Sitting down to hide his aroused state, he motioned to the chairs in front of his desk. Her skirt rose up when she sat, awarding him a glimpse of black lace panties before she crossed one leg over the other. When he met her gaze again, it was evident she knew what he'd seen. Planned it even, perhaps. He leaned his arms on the desk, attempting to maintain some sort of professional demeanor.

"To what do I owe the pleasure?" he tried again, biting back a groan as she placed her elbows on the desk as well, leaning forward to give him a very clear view of her creamy breasts. Her nipples poked enticingly at the front of her outfit, and he nearly shivered at the thought of how they'd taste on his tongue. Swallowing hard, he stared into her eyes. "Should I prepare the chapel? Do we have a wedding to perform?" Thankfully his voice didn't shake as much as his legs were under the desk.

Betsy licked her lips slowly, the corners stretching up into a smile. "Come on, Ian - don't you want to play? Talk dirty to me." Her words were enticing, but her eyes reflected something more serious. Worry, maybe even fear. He leaned back, regarding her thoughtfully.

"Something's wrong," he said, knowing he was right when her lips dropped into a serious line. "You know you and Harley are my family - you can tell me anything. What's going on?"

She looked down then, settling back in her chair and nervously playing with the tiny lace apron she wore. "I--well, there was this guy tonight at the Mansion," she said, her gaze darting around the room. "I got a call last week, and it's probably not related, but I thought I should tell someone just in case, but I knew Harley would overreact, and--"

"Hey," he said, coming around the desk against his better judgment. He pulled the second chair to face her and sat down, reaching out to grasp her hand. A jolt of warm energy infused his skin the second they touched, but he focused on the worried green eyes finally focused back on him. "Just tell me, it's okay. Did you sleep with him?" *Please say no.*

"No! It's nothing like that, I just..." She yanked her hand out of his, launching out of her chair to pace at the side of his desk. "Last week, my lawyer called to tell me that Derek was up for parole. They let him out two days ago." She stopped, inhaling deeply then letting it out in a long shaky sigh.

That would explain why her hands were shaking so badly, Ian noted. Her ex-husband had tried to kill her five years ago, and had been sent to prison for attempted manslaughter. He'd promised to finish the job when he got out, but no one had expected him to be granted parole. No wonder she was afraid. He rose, walking over to fold her in his arms.

"I'm so sorry, Bets," he said, wishing he could do something to ease her worries. "We need to let Harley know, just in case he...well, just in case."

She pulled back a little, looking up at him with such anguish it broke his heart. "That's the thing, Ian. I think I saw him tonight. At the Mansion. I think he's here already." Tears fell down her cheeks as she buried her face in his chest, her fingers holding on to his shirt as if her life depended on it.

Holding her tight with one arm, Ian picked up the phone on his desk with the other. He pressed "zero", then waited, slowly rocking Betsy side to side as she clung to him.

"You've reached the voice mail of Harley Majors. Leave a message and I'll call you back as soon as I can." A long beep sounded in his ear.

"Harley, this is Ian. Listen, Derek Taft is out of jail, and your sister thinks she saw him here tonight, on the ranch. Get back to me as soon as possible - Betsy's with me." He hung up, then gently untangled her fingers from his shirt so he could step back, needing to put some distance between them so he could think. "How sure are you that it was Derek? Is there any chance it could have just been someone who looked like him?"

She sunk into a chair, taking the tissue he handed her and wiping her nose. "I don't know," she said, shaking her head and staring out the window behind him. "It really looked a lot like him, but I can't be sure. I just...froze when I saw him, then I panicked and came straight to you." She looked up at him, pleading with her eyes. "I didn't know what else to do."

"It's okay," he said, unable to resist running a finger down the side of her face. "I won't let anything happen to you, you know that, right?"

She turned into his touch, closing her eyes and placing a soft kiss in the palm of his hand. "I know," she whispered, taking his hands as she rose from the chair. "You've always looked after me, Ian. I knew I could count on you." Placing a hand on his shoulder she stood on her tiptoes and pulled his head down just a little, placing a quick kiss on his cheek. Then another on his jaw. And one on his chin.

Ian knew he should stop her, knew he shouldn't encourage her. But so help him, when she pressed her lips tentatively to his, he didn't pull away. And when she flicked her tongue against his lower lip, teasing him for more he pulled her roughly against his chest, opened his mouth and gave what she asked for.

She tasted sweet, the innocent flavor of bubble gum mixing with the mild tingle of her peppermint lip gloss. Then again, forbidden fruit always was sweeter, he thought as he explored every inch of her mouth with his tongue. Ignoring his conscience, he kissed down the column of her long, slender neck. She urged him on, running her fingers through his hair and he gladly moved lower still, pulling the collar of her dress down to expose one pretty, pert breast. He laved around the aureole with his tongue then sucked the pebbled nub between his lips, earning a shocked gasp.

"Oh Ian, yes. Right there - so good..."

He glanced up and her head had fallen back, her skin taunt and glowing under his ministrations. In the dim light from the lamp, she looked like an angel, sent from heaven as a gift just for him. She lifted her head, smiling down on him with half-closed eyelids, those long lashes nearly sweeping over her cheeks as she held his gaze. Taking his head in both of her hands, she pulled him up for another long, hot mind-bending kiss. Then pulling back just far enough to put a scant inch between them, she whispered against his lips.

"Fuck me, Ian."

A glass of cold water wouldn't have been more effective, Ian thought, as her choice of words reminded him of just how different they really were. He pulled back and turned away, taking a few deep breaths in order to compose himself. This next part wasn't going to be fun and if he knew Betsy, she was about to throw a fit.

"I'm sorry," he started, not turning around just yet. "I should never have done that. I shouldn't have betrayed your trust or given in to my baser instincts. Forgive me?"

He turned around, surprised that she hadn't jumped in yet, but she was nowhere in sight. Gone.

Mixed emotions swam through his veins as he grabbed his cell phone off the desk and a jacket from the coat rack and ran out the door. What if Derek was really at the ranch? She was out there alone somewhere, and it was all his fault. He vowed then and there not to let her out of his sight again.

* * *

Hot tears fell as Betsy ran across the compound, humiliation and sadness pressing so tightly in her chest that it was hard to breath. She'd known the second the words passed her lips that she'd gone too far. How could she have been so stupid, thinking Ian would just fall into her arms, forgetting everything in her past life? It wasn't his religion holding him back, she knew. He wasn't bound by any vows of celibacy, but he was a good man. Honorable. And sleeping with someone like her...well. She imagined it wouldn't look all that great to his peers, much less his God. He was probably praying for forgiveness right now, along with salvation for her poor, misguided soul.

A little voice in the back of her head told her she was being unfair, striking out at him because she was angry. Ian wasn't that kind of man. But the fear and indignity pervading her thoughts were louder, and as she stumbled through the back door of the mansion she vowed to stay away from him from that point forward. She was done. Finished.

Making her way down to the sub-basement where she and Harley lived, she toed off her heels and swiped at her eyes as she walked the long corridor to her suite. A noise from the other end of the hall kicked her heart rate up and she froze, turning around slowly. Had Derek found a way down here somehow? Suddenly the walls seemed to close in as steady footsteps shuffled closer. She backed away, wondering if she could lock herself in her rooms before he reached her. She glanced over her shoulder to check the distance, just as the footsteps stopped.

"Betsy? Are you okay?"

The familiar female voice made her want to weep with relief. She nodded, suddenly self-conscious in front of her sister-in-law, but thankful to see her all the same. "I...yes," she said, not sure how much of the evening she wanted to admit to. Harley had married Monica recently just to keep her safe from her overbearing father, and in light of what they were going through, her own problems seemed paltry. She laughed nervously, blinking quickly to disperse the tears. "Just some guy trouble," she said, waving it off with one hand. "You know how men are."

Monica nodded, a thoughtful look on her face. "Yes I do," she said quietly. "Come on, let's talk."

"It's kind of messy," Betsy said as they reached her door, sliding the key into the lock. I've been working extra shifts lately, and--" Something cold and hard poked her stockinged foot and she looked down, spying a manila envelope with a brass clasp. "What's this?"

Monica shrugged. "Were you expecting something?"

Betsy frowned, turning the envelope over to check for a label. It was blank.

"No," she said, bending the metal tabs up and lifting the flap. "No one else is supposed to be down here, not even the staff. If you didn't leave it..." She held the sides apart so she could peer in at the single sheet of paper. Sliding it out, she stared down at the image for a moment, her mind refusing to process what it was seeing.

Monica reached for the page, gasping as she took in the meaning. "Lock the--wait, this was inside the door, right?" Betsy nodded, still stunned. "Come on," Monica said, grabbing her hand and tugging her quickly back out into the hall. She slammed the door behind them and pulled Betsy away from her suite. "Whoever left that could still be in there...we need to call Harley." They reached the suite that Harley and Monica shared and locked themselves inside. Only then did Monica pull her cell phone out of her pocket.

"Maybe it's just a practical joke," Betsy offered as she perched on a stool at the kitchen counter, unable to take her eyes off the page. The words sounded flat even to her own ears, and Monica took the paper from her and turned it face down on the counter.

"Harley, it's me," she said into the phone, her hand still firmly over the page. "We have a serious problem - you need to come home right away." She paused, and Betsy could imagine the hassle her brother was giving his wife over her demand. He'd always been stubborn, and while there was definitely something between the two of them, neither seemed willing to admit it yet.

"Want me to talk to him?" she said quietly. Monica shook her head, then looked back down at the floor. "Harlan Majors, get your ass down here right now. There's something you need to see." She disconnected the call and tossed her phone on the counter, letting out a long sigh as she rubbed her forehead. "Was he always this pigheaded?"

Betsy met her gaze with a sympathetic look. "Worse, I'm afraid. He's always wanted to do exactly the opposite of what anyone tells him to do, which made for some interesting high school days." She grinned. "Not many people have the balls to talk to him like that though. I'll bet for you, he's on his way down."

Chapter Two

Right on cue, Betsy heard the front door open and slam shut. Harley came around the corner two seconds later, a scowl on his face as he glanced from one to the other, finally settling on Monica. "What the hell is going on? Why didn't you tell me Betsy was here?" He shifted to include Betsy. "Ian left a message saying Derek might be here at the ranch, is that true? Why didn't you tell me he was out?"

Betsy shook her head, blinking back a fresh set of tears. "I was going to tell you about Derek, but you've been so busy with getting married and all - I didn't want to distract you. Then I thought I saw him tonight and sort of freaked out, so I went to Ian's but we had a fight and I came home and that's when I found this." She flipped the paper over and slid it in front of him. "Monica was with me and wanted to call you so here we are."

Harley stared down at the image, his phone jangling from his pocket. Without taking his eyes off the page, he held the phone up to his ear and answered with a terse, "Yeah."

Betsy couldn't stop herself from taking just one more peek at the grotesque image that would undoubtedly haunt her dreams for a long time to come. It was a picture of her, taken recently in the same French maid outfit she still had on, so whoever had gotten it either was here or had been. Whoever left it had photo-shopped her image with a noose around her neck, hanging from the barrister of the grand double staircase on the main floor. Her wrists looked like they'd been slit, and her blood pooled on the floor below.

"We're all in my suite, Ian...come on over." Harley disconnected the call and shoved the phone down in his front pocket. Looking thoughtfully at Betsy, he reached across the counter and took one of her hands. "He sounds pretty bad, sis - what were you fighting about? Did you hit on him again?"

"I'm sure it doesn't matter," Monica said. Betsy shot her a grateful look. "Whatever the problem, I'm sure they'll get over it--"

Harley shook his head, a chuckle of disbelief escaping. "Darlin', you don't know what you're talking about. Why don't you run upstairs and make sure our guest isn't foaming at the mouth because I'm not there. I'll be up as soon as I'm done here."

Betsy's heart broke for her new sister-in-law. Ashamed, she pulled her hand out of Harley's. "Harlen Majors." No woman deserved to be treated like that. Harley's expression softened and he reached for Monica, but she ran out of the kitchen. Betsy didn't blame her. "You should go after her," she said, knowing he wouldn't, but needing to say it. "That was uncalled for and you know it. She just wanted to help."

He met her gaze, his expression one of hurt and resignation. "I'll talk to her later. Your safety is more important right now. When did Derek get out of prison?" The front door opened and shut, and she tried to brace herself, knowing it could only be one person.

"A couple weeks ago. Look, I know I should have told you, but--" she stopped, the words caught in her throat as Ian appeared in the doorway behind Harley. Their eyes met, briefly, but she looked away, unable to face the regret in them. Her face flamed as the minister rounded the counter to stand beside her.

Harley pushed the photo across the counter to Ian. "Someone left this under her door. We need to get her out of here, at least until I can figure out what's going on with Derek."

Ian nodded. "I'll take her. We can be gone in an hour." He grabbed the photo and flipped it over, hot, angry vibes coming off his body in waves.

"I don't want to go anywhere," Betsy said quietly, her eyes on the stone counter top. "If I run, he wins."

"If you run, you stay alive," Harley countered. "I've got all sorts of crap going on here right now, and Derek is just one more thing. I'll find him, and I'll make sure he doesn't bother you again, but you have to get out of here so I won't be worried about you every second of the day." He curled a hand over Ian's shoulder. "I really appreciate this. I don't care where, and I don't need to know, just find somewhere safe to hole up for a week or so. Charge it to the ranch."

"But I--" Betsy stood up, ready to fight. How dare they pass her around like some errant child in need of babysitting! She trembled where she stood, her muscles tied in knots of anger and frustration.

Harley held his hand up, giving her a stern look. "He's the only one I trust to take care of you, sis. Don't argue. Just go." He walked around the counter and gave her a quick hug, then headed for the door, pausing to glance back over his shoulder. "Don't give him any trouble, Bets. This is serious." Without waiting for an answer, he walked out, leaving her alone with her fear and the one man who could only make things worse.

Betsy bit her lower lip as the door slammed behind Harley. Keenly aware of Ian's presence, she didn't dare look his direction. Her face burned with embarrassment, not just because of what happened earlier in his office, but for being passed off on him like some recalcitrant child. Could this day get any more humiliating?

"You know he's right," Ian said, with none of the censure she'd expected in his tone. "There's no shame in staying safe."

She shook her head. He didn't understand. No one did. There was a reason Derek had tried to kill her before, aside from the alcohol problem everyone had blamed his actions on. He wouldn't stop hunting her until he got what he wanted, or until she was dead, preferably both. A chill settled in the base of her spine at the thought.

"You don't get it," she said quietly, pretending to examine her chipped French manicure. "He won't stop until he finds me. He can't."

"Tell me." It wasn't a request, it was a command. Ian stepped closer, hooking a finger under her chin and lifting her head to look at him. "It's important that I know what we're dealing with if I'm going to protect you."

She pulled away, turning the stool and sliding off so she could put some distance between them. "I...we did some things, Derek and I, that I'm not proud of. And some of them resulted in a lot of money that we hid in offshore accounts. We put them under my name, because he was sure the government was watching him. Probably paranoia from the alcohol and drugs. Derek always worried about our 'electric money' disappearing, so little by little we exchanged it for gold coins. He said he always wanted to know what a real chest full of treasure would look like." She shook her head, the story sounding cheesy even to her own ears.

"We'd take enough money out of the bank for a few coins, and buy them a couple at a time so no one would get suspicious. He had a woodworker make him a wooden chest, and we'd put the coins in there. He even hid it in a cave on his property, even though I warned him it could all easily just disappear. But he was caught up in the pirate-like reality he'd created for himself."

Ian shifted behind her, and Betsy turned to see him leaning against the counter, watching her thoughtfully. "How did you do it?" he asked quietly.

She shrugged. "He was losing touch with reality more each day, drinking enough to forget. So I started taking a few coins here and there, thinking I'd need some money when I finally got the courage to leave. Then I left, and after he found me and almost killed me..." she met Ian's hard stare straight on. "I felt like I deserved the rest."

He nodded, his expression blank as he looked at the photo on the counter. "Where is it now?"

"In the tunnels," she said, referring to the maze like warren that ran beneath the ranch. "And if it was just the money, I'd give it back, though it wouldn't stop him from killing me. But there's something else..." she stopped, unwilling to put all her secrets on the line. Maybe it wouldn't be necessary, if they could just keep Derek away from her hiding spot.

"What else? I need to know everything." Ian stepped closer, his nearness intimidating even as it made her want to lean into his warmth.

She shook her head. "We just need to keep him away from that chest. If we can do that, what's in it doesn't matter."

* * *

Ian turned away, barely resisting the urge to shake Betsy senseless. "Come on," he said, turning back to face her. "I need you to be transparent with me. If you don't trust me..."

She shook her head, anguish in those big green eyes. "If it were just me affected, I'd tell you in a heartbeat. But there's someone else involved, and the less people who know anything about it, the better. Just let it go, Ian. Please." She tilted her head to the side and he shook his head at her pleading stare.

"Fine. I'll let you have your secret for now. Will you at least tell me where you hid the chest? We should make sure Derek hasn't gotten to it already."

She bit her lower lip again, her gaze shifting to the floor. "Well, I would. The thing is, I'm not sure exactly where it is."

"You're kidding, right?" Ian threw his hands up in frustration. "If we don't know where it is, how the heck are we going to find it? How do you forget where you hid a chest full of money?"

Betsy shrugged. "I said it was in the tunnels. I brought it here, but I wasn't the one who actually hid it. A friend and I...um, were drinking in my suite one night and talking about how funny it was that Derek thought he was a pirate. I showed her the chest. When I passed out, she hid it somewhere in the tunnels as a practical joke. She was leaving for Europe the next day, and was on a plane before I realized the chest wasn't in my closet anymore."

Ian closed his eyes briefly, rubbing his nose. "So where is your friend now? How do we get a hold of her?"

"Last I heard she was on her way to Africa. She loves to travel, and rarely stays in one place for long. Unfortunately it's pretty hard to actually get a hold of her, so I lost touch with her awhile back. I have no idea how we'd reach her now. But there's another way to find the chest, I think."

"I'm all ears," Ian said, leaning against the counter. He was beginning to wonder if the whole story was just something Betsy made up. It sounded far too fantastical to be real, but he couldn't afford not to take it seriously, just in case even part of it was true.

She paced in front of him, hugging her arms to her chest as she avoided his gaze. "Keep in mind that we'd had a lot to drink," she said, her cheeks coloring a rosy hue. "And this place tends to get to you, with all the fantasy themes. When you consider both of those, it's really not that surprising--"

"Just spit it out."

"My friend made a map so I could find the chest when I needed to. A...um...well, a treasure map, sort of. It's a list of clues that lead to the...uh, treasure, so to speak."

Ian shook his head again, a long sigh escaping as he straightened. "Let me get this straight. Your ex was so delusional that he hid coins in a wooden chest, which you then stole. You got drunk one night with a friend who hid the treasure and left you what amounts to a map? Do you have any idea how crazy all this sounds? How do you know your friend didn't take the chest with her? Where does she get all that traveling money?"

Betsy punched him in the arm. "She's a sociologist, so she gets grant money for traveling. And she wouldn't just steal from me like that. We were best friends, dammit. I thought you were supposed to trust people, being a preacher and all."

"You never looked for the money though? Weren't you just a little concerned?"

She shrugged again. "Not really. I wasn't going to spend it anyway, I was saving it for retirement. I figured it was probably safer wherever it was than in my closet, so..."

Ian rubbed his neck. "So you want to stay here, where a killer is after you, to protect a chest that you're not even sure is here anymore." She nodded, and he continued. "If we can prove the chest isn't here, will you let me take you somewhere safe?"

"I guess so."

He sighed again, running a hand through his hair. He should get her out of there now, money and secrets aside. But knowing her, she'd just find a way to come back without him, putting herself in even more danger.

"Okay," he said, holding out a hand. "Let's get the map."

* * *

Betsy followed Ian down the long, dim hall, past the elevator shaft and the entrance to the tunnels. When they finally reached the door to her suite, he put a finger to his lips and motioned for her to stand against the wall beside the door. He pushed the door open slowly, and Betsy couldn't help but think that it should be Harley with her, checking out her place to make sure it was safe. At least he carried a gun. What was Ian going to do if he found someone? Pray for him?

She shifted her stance, the cold from the polished cement floor seeping into her stocking feet. Glancing down at herself, she shook her head. She'd need to change out of the tiny French maid costume before they went anywhere. Jeans and a t-shirt would be much more appropriate for crawling around the dirt tunnels.

Ian poked his head around the door frame. "It looks clear - come on." He disappeared just as quickly, and she followed him inside, closing the door behind her. When she turned, it was all she could do not to collapse right then and there in defeat.

"Whoa," she breathed, trying to comprehend the magnitude of the chaos before her. She wasn't a neat freak by any stretch of the imagination, but still. She'd never trash a room this badly. At least not on purpose. "He was here, wasn't he?"

"Looks that way. Even you aren't this messy." Ian grinned at her, clearly trying to lighten the mood. She rubbed her arms, fear and cold creeping under her skin like some parasite. She couldn't move, could barely breath. Why couldn't Derek just stay in prison like he was supposed to?

His smile fading, Ian moved in front of her, blocking the view and momentarily breaking the paralyzing effect. "Hey, it's gonna be okay." He pulled her into his embrace, hugging her briefly before stepping back and squatting down a little to look her in the eye. "We can't stay here, Bets - we need to move quickly. Do you know where the map is?"

She nodded, forcing herself to focus. "I have a floor safe in the bedroom. It's in there." She brushed past him and headed for the hallway, then stopped when she realized he was following her. Turning

around, she shook her head. "You wait out here. I
need to change clothes while I'm at it."

"No." Ian shook his head.. "I'm not letting you
out of my sight - he could be hiding anywhere. I
won't look, but I'm coming in with you."

She shrugged, wondering what would happen if
he did peek. Good things for her, no doubt. "Suit
yourself." Continuing to her bedroom, she considered
changing first, but the chance to show the good rev-
erend what he was missing was too good to pass up.

Moving the nightstand over a foot or so, she
knelt down and pried up a couple loose floorboards.
Leaning over and giving Ian a great, unobstructed
view of her ass as her uniform slid up, she took her
time putting the combination in. Finally she swung
the door up, and took out a folded sheet of paper.

"Got it!" she said, holding it up triumphantly as
she turned around.

Ian was gone.

Chapter Three

"If you can't stand the heat, stay out of the fire!" Betsy yelled toward the doorway Ian had been standing in just moments before. Shaking her head, she went to the closet and hurried into her favorite pair of jeans, a long-sleeved t-shirt, socks and good cross-trainers. Dressed more appropriately for creeping around in dirt tunnels, she grabbed the map off the bed where she'd left it and went to find Ian.

As she made her way to the living room, she mused at how her mood had turned around. Circumstances being what they were, she was surprised to realize it was excitement building in her stomach, rather than fear. At least until she saw the two men standing in front of her fireplace. It was definitely fear that made her insides turn then, and she approached cautiously.

"About time you joined us, Bets," Derek said, holding Ian at gunpoint and looking pointedly at the paper in her hand. "I assume that's the map your friend drew? You just be a good girl and hand that over, and I'll let your boyfriend here live."

"Run, Betsy," Ian hissed, only to earn an elbow in the side that doubled him over. Betsy clenched the paper harder, looking down to find an entire corner crinkled, with a small tear half-way up the page. Had *she* done that?

She shook her head. "You'll just kill him anyway. I'm not going anywhere. And I'm not giving you the map either."

Derek laughed. "I figured you'd be difficult. Why don't I just take care of your friend here, and you and I will go find the treasure together. Hell, maybe if you're good, I'll give you a second chance. I wouldn't mind you warming my bed again..."

He stepped back a little and raised the gun higher, so it was pointed dead center at Ian's chest. Betsy knew he was just crazy enough to pull the trigger.

"No!" She rushed forward and he turned the gun toward her, squeezing off a shot at nearly the same time she tripped on a rug and fell to the floor. When she looked up, she saw Ian tackle Derek from the side, and both men went down as another shot rang out. Staying low, she crawled behind the couch as the gun slid across the floor from the other side. She shoved it under the couch and pushed to her feet just as Ian grabbed her wrist and pulled her toward the door.

Running behind Ian, she was nearly out in the hall before something tugged hard on the paper in her other hand. Horrified, she heard the sound of paper ripping as Ian yanked her across the threshold and pulled the door shut, then set off down the hall at what seemed like top speed. His grip on her wrist was like a steel manacle and she had no choice but to keep moving or she'd fall on her face. It was impossible to hear whether Derek was following them or not, but she risked a quick glance back as Ian pulled her into the stairwell that lead down to the tunnels and the passage was clear.

"He got part of the map," she gasped when Ian finally stopped to open the access door. She stepped inside when it swung open and automatically reached for the flashlight kept just inside every tunnel entry. When the door clicked shut, she switched on the light and pointed it toward the torn paper in her hand. "Dammit. He's got the whole first half."

* * *

"Come on," Ian said, starting down the tunnel. "Let's worry about a place to hide first, and then we'll figure out what to do about the map."

His broad back had already disappeared into the pitch black beyond when Betsy finally looked up, and she swung the flashlight his way as she hurried after him. Grateful she'd changed clothes, she tried to keep pace with his long stride, her tennis shoes scuffing across the dirt floors.

She followed as Ian veered sharply to the right, then left before going straight until they came to a smaller wooden door that looked as old as the ranch.

"Where are we going?" she asked as she watched him struggle with the key for a moment. The door finally swung open, and she shined the flashlight into the older parts of the warren underneath the ranch. She'd never been down that far - Harley had always said it was unsafe. He and Ian had scouted them out when they'd first moved in, and while there were plans to eventually have an entire suite of guest areas down here, they were still working on expansion plans.

"Not too much farther," he said, closing the door and locking it before he led the way forward. "I have a place up ahead - kind of a hideout, I guess. Harley and I fixed up one of the rooms for when we needed to just sort of hide for awhile. I think it turned out pretty nice, myself." He took a left down a short corridor, stopping at yet another door near the end. "Here we are." He pushed the door open and stepped back, gesturing for her to go first.

Betsy trained the single beam of light in her hand through the doorway, moving slowly into the room. Swinging the light in a wide arch, she was impressed by all the furniture the guys had managed to bring down. A couch, several chairs, even what looked like a queen sized mattress.

"Wow, you really put a lot of work into this." A click sounded behind her, followed by a gentle hum and as she turned to face Ian, dim lanterns came on all around the room, bathing everything in a gentle white glow. "Nice touch," she added, smiling at him.

He tilted his head in acknowledgment. "Thank you. The generator runs off the low current in the stream, so we don't have to haul gasoline. We also have it attached to a solar panel up above - the ceiling isn't all that thick here, which makes it easy to punch holes in, but there's a certain amount of risk with that too. Don't want the whole thing to cave in..."

He was so cute talking about generators and solar panels, Betsy thought as she flipped off the flashlight. So much more relaxed than normal, even though they were technically supposed to be on the run by now. She laid their half of the treasure map on a round wooden table nearby, and set the flashlight on top of it. Then she turned to him and shook her head.

"I know I'm supposed to leave you alone, and dammit, I tried. But you're just so...so..." Preparing herself for rejection yet again, she advanced on him, and to her surprise he stood his ground. "You know this is going to happen, right?" she practically whispered the words, but it was clear from his expression that he'd heard just fine. "We don't have a choice, Ian. You may as well just get over it, because this...thing, between us?" She smoothed a shaking hand up over his chest, the fabric of his shirt rough against her palm. "It's meant to be."

* * *

Ian chuckled and turned away, glad the room was relatively dim even with the lights. The thing is, Betsy was right. They'd been working their way towards this since they were sixteen, and even when he'd taken that online course to become a minister to perform weddings at the ranch, he'd still known it was only a matter of time.

Small hands caressed his back, moving up to lightly massage his shoulders. He closed his eyes, trying to remember all the reasons he had to say no. Harley, Derek, the missing so-called treasure, the fact that his heart would be torn in two by morning...

Those long fingers slid down his back, then snuck around his waist as Betsy embraced him from behind. Her breasts pressed close against his back, and his hands moved over her arms of their own accord. Something else moved too, below his belt, making his jeans more than a little uncomfortable. Then she moved one hand lower, her fingers deftly flicking his fly open, and it was too late. Her nails just barely skimmed his cock over his standard-issue briefs, and the traitor twitched neatly against her hand, clearly begging for more. The only thing standing between him and embarrassment at how much he wanted her was remembering all the times she'd begged him, and he'd turned her down.

Not tonight. Not anymore.

He grasped her wrist and pulled her around to face him. Her eyes shone up at him in the amber glow, a jumble of mixed emotions laid out bare for him to see. Fear. Longing. Worry. Excitement.

She opened her mouth, and he dipped his head to capture her lips before she could speak.

Her low moan vibrated through his body as he crushed her tight to his chest. Teasing her with his tongue, he lapped and suckled and tasted, giving her everything she asked for, matching her thrust for thrust. When he finally pulled back just a scant couple of inches, she blinked, her gaze unfocused as she swayed in his arms.

"Wow," she breathed, leaning into him for support. "We should have done that a long time ago."

Ian shook his head. "Nah. Wouldn't have been as good." He eased her into standing on her own, zipped up his pants and then tugged at her hand. "Come on. I want to show you something."

"I sure hope it's what I think it is," Betsy teased as they walked across the cavern. Ian grinned, pulling her through a narrow passage hidden behind a grandfather clock. Just before the cavern ended, he turned around, blocking her view.

"Cover your eyes," he said, waiting until she complied. "Now don't look until I tell you, okay?"

She nodded, and he took her arm, leading her the last few steps to paradise. "Now you can look."

At first, she just blinked, trying to get her bearings. Ian watched her face as comprehension grew. Her lips rounded in awe, her eyes darting every which way. She looked up, examining the ceiling as she moved farther into the room and he could guess what she was thinking.

"The cavern was open to the sky for a long time - an earthquake, we think. That gave the vegetation time to take over, and then the previous owner designed a new retractable cover for the place. From the outside, it looks like just another rise in the earth.

She turned to him and grinned. "This is great, Ian. But there's something else that rises I'd rather see just now..."

* * *

Sliding her arms around his neck, Betsy stood on her tip-toes to offer Ian a kiss. Her heart nearly burst with joy as he leaned down to indulge her, his hands slipping around her rib cage. This is what she'd wanted for so long, what she'd pined for even when she was with other men. Ian was the man she'd wanted all her life, and now, finally his mouth was on hers, nibbling at her lips as if she were a piece of gourmet chocolate.

He traced her jaw line, sucked her earlobe and placed tiny kisses down her neck, one after another sending ripples of pleasure through her body. Then his arms tightened around her like a vise, clamping her hard against his chest and she frowned as a loud rattling sound echoed off the chamber walls. The hair stood up on the back of her neck and she struggled, desperate to see what was behind her and fearing the truth at the same time.

"Don't move," Ian whispered, his hot breath tickling her ear. "There's a rattlesnake about three feet behind you. If we move wrong, we're dead."

Betsy closed her eyes, freezing in place. Not that she had much choice, the way Ian was holding her. "You mean I'm dead," she whispered, clinging to his neck yet balancing on her toes, not wanting to pull him over with her weight.

"I won't let that happen."

There was no hesitation in his voice, no question that he would keep her safe at all costs, and despite the venomous reptile behind her, Betsy relaxed just a little.

"So what's the plan?" she asked, fighting the curiosity that made her want to turn around and face her attacker. Her fingers curled into his shirt, digging into the skin on his shoulders until she realized what she was doing, and forced herself to ease her grip.

"Sorry," she said, looking sheepishly up at him from beneath her lashes. His focus was on a point somewhere beyond her though, and she wondered if he'd even felt her nails.

"We need to back away very slowly. The entrance to the passage out is right behind me. On three, I want you to relax your toes - I'll carry you over there."

Betsy gave her head a shake, freezing when she saw Ian's stern look. "I'm too heavy. We'll fall, and the snake will strike, and..."

"Trust me."

He didn't give her a count. One second she was standing there staring at him, the next her feet were off the ground, swinging around as he switched places with her and then ran for the opening in the rock. Betsy hung on for dear life until he finally put her down just inside the passage entrance. She looked past him to the clearing they'd just left.

"Looks like it left," she said, squinting in the dim light as she tried to find the errant reptile. "Now how do we avoid running into him again?"

Chapter Four

Still shaken, Betsy tried to stay focused as Ian stepped into the narrow space beside her and took the lantern. His distinctly male scent and the heat coming off his body made her want to grab him and pick up where they left off, but the idea that the snake might come back made her hesitate.

"I doubt it will venture far from this cavern," Ian said, his voice soothing. "There's a stream that runs through the vegetation in the back, and animals are pretty smart about staying near water. Still, it's probably not a good idea to stay in the clubhouse after all. Might be a little too close for comfort."

"I agree," Betsy said, stepping back into the furnished underground room. "Just let me get the map, and..." She stopped, nearly stumbling forward as Ian ran into her from behind.

"Nice of you to join me," Derek said, one hand brandishing a gun, the other holding up their half of the map that Betsy had left on the table. "Now that we're all together, and have a complete map again, why don't we sit down and talk about this whole mess." He pointed in the direction of the couch with his gun, and Betsy walked over and took a seat, not knowing what else to do. Ian sat beside her, close enough that their thighs were touching. Appreciative of the support, she tried to ignore his proximity as Derek's glance flicked between the two of them. Tired, cranky and wound tight with sexual tension, she threw caution to the wind and looked her ex straight in the eye.

"Why don't you just kill us?"

Derek propped one hip on the table and shrugged. "I don't know the ranch as well as you two, for one thing. This little treasure hunt will go faster with inside help. And then there's the little matter of those papers - if I recall correctly, I need your signature before I'll be able to do anything with them."

She shook her head. "You'll never get it. You might as well just kill me now. I'll be damned--"

"Now, now. Settle down." He calmly moved the gun to train it on Ian. "That's where he comes in. I know all about your little crush - I did my research. And I'm betting you'll do anything to protect this guy, right?" He paused, raising an eyebrow when she didn't immediately answer. "Or maybe not. Tell me now, darlin' - if you don't want him around, I'll take care of him right here. Then it will be you and me alone together, just like old times."

"You're right," she said, aware of Ian tensing beside her, but unwilling to see how far Derek was willing to take this. He wasn't a rational man, no matter how it appeared, and she was positive he wouldn't hesitate to kill Ian to make a point. "I do have a crush on him, I have since I was fifteen. Please don't kill him." She hated the pleading note in her voice, but at least this time she'd put it there for a reason. She wasn't the naive girl he'd married. And if she had to play his game to get them both out safely, that's what she'd do, despite the disapproval she could feel from Ian.

Derek looked at her, his gaze boring into her soul. For a long moment she was sure he'd kill Ian anyway, just to hurt her. But finally he released her with a nod.

"Now that we all understand our roles, let's start with the first clue." He glanced down at the paper in his hand, his eyes skimming over the page. "Treasures of the flesh will lead you to the first coin."

* * *

Derek looked up from the map. "The first coin? What the hell does that mean - they're all hidden separately?" He banged a hand down on the table, the loud noise making Betsy jump. Angry and frustrated, she pushed off the couch and marched over to stand in front of him. Deliberately ignoring the gun he pressed against her belly, she pointed to the very top of the page.

"Seriously. Do men ever read the instructions? It says right here that she left a coin at each place to mark the spot, and the chest is at the last place. Since I know you're going to ask why we can't just jump straight to the last clue, I'll just point out that most of the directions after this one are actual travel directions, with a clue to help find the coin. So I'd suggest you actually read the map before we go anywhere." Struggling not to visibly shake from the adrenaline and anger flowing through her system, she stepped back, flinching when he thrust the papers at her.

"Take 'em," he commanded when she didn't immediately reach for the two halves of the map. "You've got this whole thing figured out, so you should be able to lead the way without any trouble."

She took the map, wondering for a second if she could run fast enough...

"Don't even think about it," Derek warned, waving the gun to get her attention. Betsy tried to look defeated, aware of Ian approaching her from behind. His warm hands curled over her shoulders, the touch calming though she watched Derek's lips turn down in disgust.

"How did you find us?" Ian asked, squeezing gently, rhythmically a few times in a motion that made Betsy want to lie down on the floor and take a nap.

Derek stood up, one hand shoved into the pocket of his jeans, the other moving the gun to point at Ian. "When I got out of the joint, I heard about Betsy's betrayal first thing. A friend of mine had a dad who was in the group who used to live here - he told me about all sorts of fun places to hide around these parts. I've been sleeping down here since. It wasn't that hard to figure out where you went when you disappeared into thin air back at the mansion."

Ian's hands slipped away as he eased in front of Betsy. "That doesn't explain how you tracked us here. There are a lot of rooms and tunnels - what made you look here?"

Betsy felt something flutter against her stomach, and glanced down to see Ian pointing towards the passage they'd just left behind his back. He didn't really want her to run back there, where the snake was? Or maybe that's exactly what he wanted. She had no idea what they'd do when they got to the other cavern, but if that's what Ian wanted, she'd trust him.

"It's the only tunnel with a padlock," Derek was saying. "I stole the key from Harley's suite last week."

Betsy rattled the papers, making a show of examining the first page. "I think we need to go to the Harem first. There's a shortcut back this way..." She turned and pointed to the small passage, taking a few steps toward the opening.

Derek's laugh stopped her. "You really think I'm that stupid?" he said, shaking his head. "Or were you just not listening? I've been all through this place - there's no way out of that cavern, unless you plan to climb up the walls and go through that fancy roof."

"I know a way out," Ian said, turning to stalk off toward the rock tunnel.

"Hold it right there. We're doing this my way, and that's that."

Ian stopped, and Betsy knew by the look on Derek's face that whatever Ian had planned wasn't going to work. She watched them, waiting as they both stood motionless for what seemed like hours. Praying Ian wouldn't do anything stupid, she finally let out the breath she was holding when he lifted his hands part way and slowly turned around.

"Fine," he said, shrugging before letting his hands fall back to his side. "Whatever you want - you've got the gun."

Derek nodded. "And don't you forget it. Now let's go." He waved the gun toward the door that opened back into the tunnels. "Betsy says we've got a harem to visit."

* * *

Ian went out into the hall, holding the door open for Betsy and considering slamming it in Derek's face. The other man was right behind her though, and with the gun pointed straight at her back, Ian had no choice but to close the door and follow behind. The third time Betsy asked for directions, he offered to lead, but Derek moved ahead instead, leaving Betsy to fall back.

Ian grabbed her hand as they walked in silence, wanting to reassure her. But she pulled away, and he couldn't help but think that maybe she was disappointed in him. He should have been able to get Derek away from her, somehow. Or help her escape.

Watching her back just barely visible in the darkness, it hit him again how wrong he was for her. The right man would have taken Derek out without a second thought. Or better, he would have forced her to get on a plane and leave before it was too late. But here they were, and it was a little late for heroics.

Or was it?

A familiar marking up ahead on the right wall of the tunnel briefly flashed in his vision as the light from the torch moved over it. Automatically looking down and left, he saw the pitch black opening at the base of the wall behind a couple of large boulders. The opening was no more than two feet high and four feet wide. It would be a tight fit, but the opening dropped into a small ledge that was hidden from view, and there was a narrow path along the cavern wall that came out in a tunnel about a hundred yards away. If he and Betsy could just drop through that hole and stay quiet, Derek would never know what happened to them.

Unless he'd explored that niche too.

If it was just him, he'd risk it. But the ledge was narrow, and when he and Harley had been exploring they hadn't been able to see any kind of bottom beneath. If Betsy fell...

Looking up, he frowned when he saw Derek several yards ahead with the flashlight, but no Betsy. He searched with his eyes and started to move forward when small, strong fingers grabbed his hand and pulled him toward the crevasse. When he looked down, she held a finger to her lips just before she lowered herself to the ground and slipped inside, motioning for him to follow. He hurried behind her, blood pumping fast as she disappeared below the ledge.

Thankful to feel her beside him in the absolute blackness, he held her back when she would have moved. Feeling with his free hand until he found her face, he bent to whisper as loud as he dared.

"Don't move. Our best chance is to just stay still, and quiet."

She nodded against his hand, leaning close. He put his arm around her, marveling at how perfect she felt snuggled up against his body, even given the circumstances.

Overhead, the quick scuffle of boots in the dirt and a string of curses echoed off the tunnel walls.

* * *

Ian's heartbeat was loud in Betsy's left ear as she laid her head on his chest. Above them, Derek raged, yelling expletives and threats that she knew he'd make good on if he found them. Every muscle in her body wanted to run, to get as far away from him as she could, but Ian's arm around her shoulders anchored her to him, leaving her little choice. Even whispers might carry out of the narrow opening they'd come through, giving their position away. She just hoped Ian knew what he was doing.

Finally Derek grew quiet, and Betsy shivered against Ian's body, grateful for the gentle squeeze of his arm. At least when Derek was yelling, they knew where he was.

A beam of light flared above them, occasionally illuminating a natural rock formation, but mostly just disappearing into darkness. Then a handful of rocks and dirt flew out from the opening, missing the ledge and falling into nothingness. A curse, and then the light disappeared as footsteps scuffled away from the opening. Betsy let out the breath she hadn't realized she was holding.

"I hope you're dead, but if I find you, bitch, you're going to wish you were. And that's a promise." Derek's voice rang strong, echoing in the open space. When it finally faded away, she listened, the silence complete save Ian's steady heartbeat in her ear.

A couple of minutes passed, and she tried to pull away, but Ian held her still. He leaned down, his lips caressing her ear as he spoke so softly even she could barely hear him.

"It could be a ploy," he said, his hot breath tickling her skin. "We need to stay still for a little while longer. Just to be sure. Can you do that?"

She tilted her head up enough to put her lips in the vicinity of where his might be. "I could be persuaded," she whispered, closing the distance and thanking her lucky stars when her kiss landed square on his mouth. He didn't hesitate, just opened for her and then she was lost in warm, wet, honeyed sensations as her tongue met and mingled with his. Her body tingled, her nipples burned, and she shifted her legs, trying to find relief from the aching want between them.

Then her whole body was shifting, sliding, and she grasped Ian's arms with both hands as gravity beckoned her over the lip of the rock.

"Ian, I'm...oh my god. Don't let go!" Fear and adrenaline shot through her veins, and instinctively she kicked her legs, stifling a scream when it just pulled her farther down.

"Shh..." Ian said, his strong fingers locking around her arms and pulling her back from the brink. "It's okay. I've got you." He gave another good tug, and she experienced a moment of weightlessness before she found herself sprawled across Ian's lap. The relief was overwhelming, considering the stories Harley had told her about the black holes he and Ian had found deep in the caves. If she'd fallen over the edge, no one would even hear her scream when she hit the bottom

Knowing only that she had to celebrate life, she felt her way up Ian's shirt to his neck, grabbed him and pulled his head down to hers for another soul-searing kiss.

Chapter Five

Ian tried to pull back, but Betsy held his head down with her hands at the back of his neck. She kissed and nuzzled his lips, tired of being put off. She wanted...needed to feel him inside her. She knew it wasn't smart, considering where they were, but she was tired of being careful. She wanted hot, fast and reckless, dammit.

"Betsy..." Ian whispered against her lips, pulling harder against her hold now. "It's not safe." She licked his lips, and he instinctively met her tongue with his own. "Stop," he said, even as he nibbled the lower lip she offered. His left arm still wrapped tightly around her back, his right hand slid down her side, his thumb brushing over her breast and across her nipple before continuing on to caress her hip. She shifted a little, careful to stay within the safety of his lap, letting her legs fall open. Ian took the hint, his fingers moving between her legs, flitting over her denim-covered mound.

Betsy moaned quietly into his mouth, lifting her pelvis against his hand to ask for more. Then he was undoing her jeans and his cold fingers slid inside, quickly finding her too-sensitive center and circling the tender nub.

"Oh god, Ian...more," she said as he nibbled at her neck. One long finger slid into her moist core, and she nearly cried out at the heady sensation. "Yes...yes...oh god, yes!"

He thrust in and out, each movement bringing his palm across her clit and bringing her closer to completion. Her hands balled up in his shirt she held on tight, riding his hand as much as she dared while he nibbled at her neck and shoulder. One more flick of the thumb and her world exploded, his mouth covering hers just in time to capture the cry she couldn't manage to hold back.

Slowly he extricated himself from her pants, and she felt...empty as she caught her breath and managed to fasten her jeans. She lay there quietly in his arms, letting her breathing slow and wondering what was supposed to happen next.

"I think it's safe to assume Derek's gone," Ian said, his voice rough and low. "We should probably go back up and continue through the tunnels. The ledge down here is slippery, and if one of us fell..."

Betsy nodded even though he couldn't see her, carefully pushing herself up to a sitting position beside him. "Okay," she said, not trusting her dry throat with more, and disappointed that he seemed to have no comment about what they'd just shared. Then again, she wasn't sure what she wanted him to say. So perhaps it was better to just pretend it hadn't happened. For now.

"How are we going to get back up there?" she asked, frowning in the darkness. "I didn't really pay attention to how I got down here, just made sure I swung in close to the wall and held on, like Harley told me to when he told me about the caverns. And without a light, I'm not sure how we even know which way to go."

"I know the way," Ian said, shuffling around beside her. "And we can use my cell phone for light when we need it." She felt the air stir around them, fairly certain that he'd gotten to his feet. "Reach up and feel for my hand." She waved her hand in the air, slowly, until finally her fingers contacted his.

Feeling for the wall at her back with the other hand, she let him pull her up, careful to keep her balance. He tugged her forward, and she followed with small steps, all too aware of the irony. "The blind leading the blind," she murmured, keeping her other hand on the wall for orientation. Ian stopped and so did she, relieved when he turned on his cell and pointed it away from them.

For a minute.

"Oh my god," Betsy breathed, looking out into the open expanse of nothingness that Ian's cell phone illuminated. There was just enough of the cave wall in one side of the beam to give a sort of orientation, but Ian's foot was balanced just barely on the ledge. One more step to the right, and he would have fallen off into space.

"Don't look out there. Look up here."

She forced herself to raise her head as he moved the light to reveal more of the wall. The texture in the rock almost looked like footholds, and Ian held out his hand to her, beckoning. She shook her head, positive there was no way she could scale that wall.

"We should go the other way," she said, refusing to look at him. "There's nothing to grab, no way to get back up."

A touch on her arm made her twitch, but she finally looked at him, expecting condescension or worse, amusement. But he only nodded, holding the phone out for her to take.

"The other way is worse, trust me," he said, pressing the phone into her hand when she didn't immediately take it. "I'll climb up, I've done it before. Then I can pull you up."

Every muscle in her body wanted to stop him, and she felt tears building up in her eyes. "No, you can't. You'll--"

"Stop." The word wasn't a request, but a command issued in a tone of voice she hadn't heard from Ian. It was strangely comforting, and if she were completely honest, a little arousing too. Realizing he was still speaking, she forced herself to pay attention.

"I'm going up. Hold the light just above me, like so." He took her hand and repositioned it to light the area he'd indicated. "As long as you keep the light just above me, I'll be fine. Stay close to the wall and don't let go."

He moved to the wall and reached over his head, his fingers latching onto a piece of rock. Betsy trembled as she watched him pull himself up, carefully placing one foot, then the other on the wall and finally starting to climb. She moved the light as he'd told her, keeping it just above him as he hugged the face of the wall, and then his arm disappeared to the side and he pulled himself onto the ledge above.

Playing the light on the underside, she was relieved when his head appeared above her.

"Go to the ladder, Bets...hold your hand up as high as you can for me."

Wishing she could stop shaking, she did as he asked, holding the phone in one hand, and reaching up with the other. His long fingers came down, down over the side of the ledge, but his arm wasn't quite long enough. She could hear him breathing in the stillness, the sound almost eerie in light of what she knew he'd say next.

"You're going to have to climb to where I can reach you."

Betsy shook her head, even though she knew he couldn't see her. "I can't. Really, Ian. You know how clumsy I am. I just--"

"You can, and you will." He leaned over the side to look at her again, and she couldn't see his eyes, but she could feel the intensity of his stare. "You can do this. You don't have a choice. Put the phone down on the ground pointing up, and then take it one hold at a time. Just two steps and I should be able to reach you. We'll get out of here, and go find your treasure before Derek does. He wants you to die - you heard him. You don't want him to win, do you?"

He was right. Betsy took a deep breath, set the phone on the ground and rubbed her sweaty hands on her jeans. Grabbing a hold above her head, she pulled herself up, setting her foot on the highest step she could manage before bearing down with all of her weight. Her other hand searched for a grip and she tried to ignore the pounding of her heart as she felt along the wall, her fingers finally settling in a wide crack. One more step up, one more pull, and her hand landed in Ian's warm, sturdy palm.

More confident with his support, she found another foothold that allowed her to shimmy up beside him and half-fall into his waiting arms.

"Good job," he said, hugging her tight as he rocked her back and forth. "I knew you could do it."

She nodded, not trusting herself to speak as she waited for her heart to slow down. Cooling down, she started to shiver, unable to stop even with Ian's body surrounding her.

"We'd better get you out of here," he said, standing up and pulling her to her feet. "I'm going to boost you up, okay?"

Once they were both back in the tunnel, he took her hand and started walking. She wasn't sure which way they were headed anymore, her brain refused to cooperate in the dark as he led her around a corner and through another passage. Then he stopped, and something scraped the ground ahead of them, sending a rush of panic through her again as she squeezed his hand.

* * *

Ian squeezed Betsy's fingers as he pulled the wooden door open. "It's okay," he said quietly, pulling her forward. "There should be a flashlight just over..." he leaned to his right and found the rough wall with his hand, then followed it down to the ground. Finally his wrist bumped a hard, square object, and he smiled. "Right here. Hang on for a second - I need both hands." He pulled out of Betsy's grasp with some effort, then opened the cooler and retrieved the flashlight, thankful it was still there. Pressing the button, he illuminated the tunnel with a beam of yellow light, momentarily blinded after how long they'd been in the dark.

"How did you know which way the door was?" Betsy asked, her voice a little calmer, though still shaky. "I've lost all sense of direction down here."

Ian shrugged. "Harley and I wanted to be prepared in case we ever got stuck down here without a light. So we practice moving around in the dark. Though I'll admit this is the first time I've done it without a guide rope. Freaky." He held out his hand and she put hers in it without hesitation.

"Sounds like a very dangerous game," she said as they started walking toward the camp. "But I would have been toast without you, so I'm glad you guys sort of trained for this."

"Me too," he said, playing the flashlight beam over the walls. "Do you still have the maps?"

"Oh shit," she said, stopping in place and pulling her hand away to pat the pockets of her jeans. "Uh, sorry. Damn. I mean, darn. Oh hell." She pulled a folded paper out of her back pocket and opened it up, chewing her bottom lip. Ian wanted to laugh as he watched her face contort, her lips mouthing a string of curses that didn't quite make it out.

"You know I only got ordained so we'd have a minister on site to do weddings, right?" he said lightly. Judging by the way her eyes widened when she looked at him, it was news. He nodded, taking the paper from her hand. "I'm no expert, of course, but I'm fairly certain God isn't going to strike you down for saying the F word now and then."

"Good. Because we only have the first half of the map. The other page must have fallen out somewhere. If I dropped it in the tunnel..."

"Then Derek probably picked it up," Ian finished, handing the paper back to her. She folded it up and stuffed it in her bra this time, an action Ian really enjoyed watching. Maybe she'd let him fish it out later. "Although you could have dropped it in the cavern, in which case it's definitely gone for good. But we won't know until we catch up with Derek, so unless you're ready to hop a plane and go hid out somewhere warm..."

She shook her head emphatically. "No way. I need to know for sure, either way. So come on." She started walking away from him, halting when she got to the end of the beam and looked back over her shoulder. "Are you coming?"

He tried not to smile, really, but he couldn't stop the slightest grin. "The harem is this way," he said, pointing a finger in the other direction.

*　*　*

"Right." Betsy switched directions and tried to ignore the smirk Ian was trying to hide. Her impulsive nature often had her turned around and headed the wrong way, so it wasn't anything new. Ian had steered her back on track many times when they were younger, but it was a little embarrassing that she still had no sense of direction after all these years. "Why don't you lead?" she suggested, stopping beside him. It came out more snarkily than she'd intended, but Ian just laughed.

"How about we just walk together," he said, holding out his hand. "The tunnel is plenty wide enough for us both."

Betsy wasn't sure why she hesitated, but it felt weird, having him volunteer for her touch in any way. Almost like a trap, for some reason. His smile faded, and he'd started to pull away when she reached for him, lacing her fingers with his. He squeezed her hand gently and pulled her closer, leaning down for a quick kiss before he started walking again. She walked beside him, so many questions running through her head that she wasn't sure where to start.

"Why don't you date?" she asked, deciding to jump right in. "You dated in high school a little, and I have it on good authority that there were plenty of girls after you in college, but I haven't seen you with anyone since I moved back. Don't you get lonely?"

Ian chuckled. "Fishing for the competition, are you?" he teased, flashing her another smile. "You'd be surprised how many women act interested, but run the other way when they see the white collar."

She glanced at his profile, and even in the dim light sensed that he wasn't telling the whole truth.

"Oh come on. You can't tell me you haven't played around a little in the back room on occasion. I mean, you're a guy. And I can't be the only woman on earth who gets turned on at the thought of shagging a preacher."

Laughing, he squeezed her hand. "Eloquently put. And I didn't say I've been celibate. You asked about dating, not sex."

"It's not the same thing?" she countered, suddenly wishing she hadn't started this. She didn't want to picture Ian making out with anyone else but her, and the thought of how many times she'd offered herself, how many times she'd been turned down...

She tried to pull her hand away, but he held tight and stopped, turning to look at her. "It's not the same thing at all," he said, coming closer. "Dating involves a lot more than just sex, don't you think?"

She shrugged, her eyes focused on his chest as he moved in another step. "I wouldn't know. Most of the guys I've been with just want to get me into bed. Dates are just an obligation, or that's how it feels."

"You've been dating the wrong guys, Bets," he said, lifting her chin up with a gentle hand. She stared into his eyes, mesmerized by the depth of feeling she saw reflected back at her.

"The right one didn't want me," she whispered, trembling against his body.

He wrapped his other arm around her waist, pulling her tight to him. "He was an idiot," he replied, and then covered her lips with his own.

Chapter Six

The kiss didn't last nearly as long as Betsy would have liked, and she licked her lips when he pulled back, loathe to open her eyes. Ian's face in shadow, she couldn't make out his expression very well, but the warm hand caressing the side of her neck was comforting.

"We really need to go," he said, letting his hand slide down her arm to take her hand again. "The harem is just up ahead, and Derek had a big head start. Besides..." he turned the flashlight up so she could see his grin. "They have beds there. Very plush."

She faked a big yawn, and then laughed, allowing him to pull her forward. "Now that you mention it, I could use a nap..."

Five minutes later, Ian motioned for her to stay back while he carefully opened another wooden door just a crack. It seemed like forever that he just stood there, quiet. Finally he opened the door wide and played the flashlight beam around the cavern, the light bouncing off shiny objects and gauzy fabric as it moved. When he finally turned on the light switch, Betsy went to his side.

"This is the first underground guest room," she said, moving farther into the space as he pulled the door shut behind him and pushed a wooden crate in front of it. "It's almost finished, and I suspect there will be quite a lot of demand for something so...private." Smiling, she climbed up on the large round bed that dominated the sunken center of the room and patted the space next to her. "Care to join me?"

Ian frowned, looking past her. "What do those gold coins look like?"

She turned, surveying the back wall, draped with silks. "They're just average coins, like you'd get from a bank or at a coin shop. Sort of a dull yellow-gold color. What do you see?" She slid off the other side of the bed, walking closer to examine the low table and chairs a couple steps up.

"There," Ian said, waiting until she turned to point at one of the scarves hanging lower on the wall. The fringe was covered in gold coins, but as Betsy leaned closer, there was one that didn't quite match the others in tone.

She reached out to touch it, bumping the faux coins with her hand. The mismatched coin fell and she snatched it up, turning it over in her hand before grinning at Ian.

"This is it. We found the first one!" She jumped up and down, throwing her arms around Ian's neck and dragging his head down for a kiss. He grinned, but the expression was short lived as the box in front of the door rattled. Betsy looked toward the door, aware that Ian was doing the same thing and they watched as the door pushed against the crate, groaning under the stress.

"I know you're in there." Derek's muffled voice came through the door before he strained against it again. "I knew you'd find the first coin. And now you're trapped." He laughed, the sound sending chills up Betsy's spine.

Betsy pointed toward the narrow spiral staircase in the corner. Ian nodded, grabbing her hand and pulling her forward. When they reached the metal stairs, she hurried up as fast and quietly as she could, not that Derek could hear. He was still pounding on the door and yelling, every thud moving the heavy crate just a little farther into the room.

When she reached the top, Betsy pushed open the trap door beneath the Sultan's Castle and pulled herself up, then waited for Ian to crawl out beside her. They lowered the door and looked around, Ian pointing to a large dresser across the room.

"That should slow him up for awhile," he said as they pushed it on top of the cavern entrance.

Betsy nodded as the floor beneath her began to vibrate with a dull thudding sound. "Just in time," she said, trying to catch her breath. she ran out of the small side room and into the large guest chamber where the mostly male guests in long togas reclined on creamy chaise lounges while staff dressed in authentic harem costumes served and doted on them. Staying to the side where hopefully no one would see them, she moved quickly along the wall until she found the office door and ducked inside, Ian close behind.

Collapsing on a distressed leather couch, Betsy pulled the map page out of her bra and unfolded it, scanning the clues as Ian sat down beside her.

"It says we need to go ten steps south, and then look behind the fabric wall." She frowned. "Which way is south? I'm horrible with compass directions. We should find a GPS."

Ian chuckled, taking the map from her. "You don't recognize the layout of the ranch?" He pointed to one of the crudely drawn squares. "This is where we are, I think. Ten steps south would be the salon, don't you think? Taking into consideration where the other buildings are located, anyway." He passed the paper back to Betsy and she peered closely at it.

"I guess," she said, folding it back up with a sigh. "Could it really be that easy?"

"She's your friend," Ian said, pushing to his feet and holding a hand out to help her up. "You said she was just hiding it for fun, right? So why would she make it hard?"

Betsy shrugged, following him to the door. "I just assumed it would be, I guess." She watched Ian open the door a crack, looking one way, then the other before motioning for her to follow. "Do you think he's strong enough to move the dresser?" she whispered, hugging the edges of the room again until they reached the main doors. She followed Ian into the hall and around the corner, nearly having to jog to keep up with his easy stride.

He shook his head as he led her down a short flight of stairs. "I doubt it, but he had a pretty big head start. I think the larger question is, why didn't he find the coin before us? And it seems awfully convenient that he showed up just when we found it, don't you think?"

"You think Derek followed us." Betsy stepped out of the building, blinking her eyes at the bright light. It felt good to be outside again, free from the stifling confines of the tunnels. The feeling was short-lived though as they counted out ten steps to the building next door and went inside.

"Yes," Ian said, almost whispering as he stopped in the narrow staff hallway. "But I doubt he got out of the harem fast enough to follow us over here, so we may have just bought some time." Somewhere down the hall a blower turned on, and the chemical stench of hair and nail products made Betsy wrinkle her nose.

"I have no idea why looking good has to smell so bad," she commented, falling into step with Ian as they went down the hall.

Ian shrugged, looking into various rooms as they passed. "I don't know, and I don't want to know. But we do need to find a wall of fabric. Any idea where that might be?"

Betsy motioned for him to follow her to the right through double doors near the end of the hall. "This is the only thing I can think of," she said, pointing to a wall where several rows of clothing hung floor to ceiling and side to side. "Alex is pretty proud of this - he bought an automated wardrobe system and turned it into this monstrosity."

"Wow," Ian said, his eyes wide. "I didn't know he was into that sort of thing. You wouldn't think a guy who does hair and makeup would be good with engines."

"It's all art," a deep voice said from behind them. Betsy jumped at the sound, her fear quickly turning to glee as she turned to see the subject of their conversation standing there with a smirk on his face. Running over to give him a hug, she smiled when he finally released her.

"Alex! I'm so glad you're here. Now that you are, maybe you can help--"

Ian cleared his throat, cutting her off. She looked over her shoulder to see him shaking his head. "I don't think that's a good idea, Bets."

She stepped back as Alex's hands fell away, and placed her own on her hips. "Why not? He takes care of these clothes, and he knows what's where. Maybe--"

"No." Ian stepped forward. "Sorry Alex, but involving you in this could be very dangerous in a very short time. It would be better if you didn't know anything. No offense."

Betsy glanced back at Alex, who shrugged. "Something tells me that your presence here is a bad sign anyway, considering Harley told us you two were gone for awhile. So you might as well let me do what I can. There seems to be a lot of odd things going on around here the past few days."

"We're looking for a coin," Betsy said, not looking at Ian. "One a friend of mine told me to look for at the wall of fabric here. It was awhile ago, so I realize it might not still be here, but if you've seen anything like that..."

"A gold coin?"

Betsy nodded.

Alex grinned. "I found one awhile back, in the pocket of a pirate costume. I put it in my office safe when no one claimed it. I'll get it for you."

Betsy winked at Ian as they followed him, but he didn't smile. When they got to Alex's office, Ian made sure the door was locked behind them. Alex moved a file cabinet to the side, then bent down to work the dial on his safe.

"Do you remember if there was anything with the coin?" Ian asked as he watched the safe door swing out.

Alex took a small envelope out of the safe and locked it back up before he handed Betsy the package. "There's a note with it, I think. It was kind of cryptic, like a scavenger hunt clue."

Betsy ripped open the envelope and handed the coin to Ian. She unfolded the small piece of paper and read the clue aloud.

"Go north and west one hundred steps, then find the king. He sees what you seek."

* * *

Ian turned the coin over, examining it as Betsy read the next clue. It was exactly the same as the first, with a few nicks in the edge of the soft metal. He pocketed it as Betsy handed over the clue, and read it for himself. Handing it back to her, he looked at Alex.

"Do you have somewhere you can go? Somewhere to lay low for awhile? There's a guy coming after us, and I doubt he'll be as nice."

Alex shrugged. "I guess, but what about the others here? I can't just leave the staff & clients. Are you sure he's headed this way?"

Betsy shook her head. "We can't be sure of anything except he was in the Sultan's Palace last. But he'll probably check the buildings on both sides."

"If I lock up early, it will look suspicious." Alex thought for a minute, then smiled. "I have an idea though. There's a similar coin in our costume props, made to look and feel like the real thing. I'll hold him off as long as I can, then hand that over at the last minute. It will buy you some time, at least."

Ian nodded slowly. "That's dangerous, but it could work. Can you put a note with it, with the opposite directions we have on it?"

Alex was already bent over his desk, scribbling on a piece of paper. "Done," he said, holding it up for them to see. "I'll call Harley too. If he could bring some muscle, maybe we can stop this guy."

"No!" Betsy held a hand up in the air, a panicked look on her face. "You can't call Harley until after Derek's been here. He can't know I'm still on the ranch.

"Some jerk is trying to catch you and you won't let me call Harley? Come on, Betsy," Alex pleaded. "I can't let someone like that just come in here without doing anything. He could hurt someone. You really want to just let that happen?"

"I--well--" Betsy stuttered, and Ian slid a hand lightly around her waist, gratified when she relaxed the tiniest bit against him.

"Call him," Ian said, pulling Betsy toward the door. "Whatever you have to do to catch this guy. We'll deal with the fallout later." Unlocking the door, he shook his head at Betsy when she looked up at him to argue. "Don't," he said, guiding her into the hall. "Let's go - we need to keep moving. He's still out there."

For a minute he thought he might have to toss her over his shoulder, but finally she moved past him, dropping her gaze. She didn't speak until they reached the front door and peered out the window.

"Which way is north west?"

He stepped up close behind her, feeling the heat radiating off her body as he pointed over her shoulder. "That way," he said, reading the signs on the facades across the street. "Looks like we're headed into the jungle, eh?"

Betsy wrinkled her nose, and he fought the urge to bend down and kiss it. "That could be awkward. Jane hates me. I sort of inadvertently slept with her boyfriend a few years ago."

Chapter Seven

"I'm not sure I want to hear that story," Ian said as they began walking toward Jungle Jane's. "I'm not sure I want to meet her boyfriend either."

Betsy glanced warily toward the Sultan's Palace, tugging on Ian's sleeve. "Should we just walk down the street? What if Derek got out? He might see us." She looked around, not really sure what she was looking for, but barely suppressing the urge to run between the two closest buildings.

"I thought we should count our steps to make sure," Ian said, looking at the palace as well. "But you're right. The clue is pretty straightforward, I think. Let's go over there," he pointed across the dirt road, "and use the ally entrance to the Jungle."

Betsy didn't need any further urging. She jogged between the Saloon and the biker bar, not stopping until she reached the narrow gravel strip in back. Ian was right beside her, and they walked quickly toward Jane's.

"So do I need to worry about you and Jane going at it with claws bared when we get inside?" Ian teased. Betsy shook her head, a small smile playing at the corner of her lips.

"I doubt that," she said, trying not to smirk. "But considering I owe her, don't be surprised if she..."

"If I what?" Jane said, materializing from the space between her building and the next as Betsy and Ian passed the corner. Betsy gasped, grabbing Ian's arm and he stepped in front of her, feet apart in a protective stance. Jane laughed, the sound too loud for Betsy's comfort.

"Damn it, Jane - what are you doing out here? And keep it quiet, will you?"

Jane looked Ian up and down, her eyes lingering here and there like she was admiring a piece of art. "I came out for a quick break," she said, clearly distracted by the man in front of her. Betsy couldn't really fault her for that. "And I'll keep quiet if you introduce me to this stunning creature. I don't believe we've had the pleasure..."

Ian pulled Betsy out from behind him and wrapped an arm around her waist, pulling her close to his side. "We have met, actually," he said, sounding a little perturbed to Betsy. "I'm the minister at the chapel. We've said hello at least a dozen times in passing, Jane."

The woman frowned, tossing her long blond hair behind her shoulder. She had to be freezing, Betsy thought, considering the thin animal-print sheath she wore that stopped at mid-thigh and tied over one shoulder.

"You're the preacher?" She looked up at Ian, staring hard at his face. "You normally wear a collar then, right?"

He nodded. Betsy wondered if he was regretting taking it off now, as Jane licked her lips.

"Obviously I should pay more attention," Jane said, running a finger down Ian's chest then licking the tip. "If you ever want to try a real woman on, give me a call, preacher-man. I'll take very good care of you."

Ian shifted nervously, and Betsy decided enough was enough. "Knock it off, Jane. We need to go inside for a minute. There's something we need to find." She moved to open the door, but Jane stepped in front, blocking her path.

"What are you looking for? And what are you willing to give me to get it?"

Betsy raised her eyebrows at Jane. "Seriously? You really want to go there with me? Let's remember who owns half of this ranch - and how many women want to take your place as..." she made air quotes with her fingers, "Queen of the Jungle." She put her hands on her hips and took a step forward, crowding into Jane's space, though the other woman didn't seem to mind. Her lips curved up in a patronizing smile, and Betsy half expected the cat to reach out and pat her on the head.

"You're only half-owner, dear. And let's not forget that Harley still doesn't know about your...seduction of my former fiance." Her eyes opened wide in mock surprise and she covered her mouth with one hand. "Oh dear. I suppose your minister didn't know either. Dreadfully sorry to have let the cat out of the bag. So to speak." She glanced past Betsy, and then frowned. "Where did he go, anyway?"

Betsy turned, wondering how she'd missed Ian leaving. "I don't know. He's probably inside, where we should be. I don't have time for this."

"You still owe me," Jane called as Betsy pushed past her and went through the door.

"Whatever," Betsy yelled back. She moved slowly in the dimly lit club, the quiet outside replaced by a cacophony of bird song, rushing water and the occasional wild animal call. Tribal drums beat out a primal melody in the background, and the air was cool and moist. As her eyes adjusted, Betsy scanned the perimeter of the main rooms, looking for a gold-colored statue of a king she remembered being near the waterfall the last time she'd come here. Of course she'd avoided the place since her falling out with Jane, so it had been a long time.

The king was gone, but she did spot Ian with one foot propped up on a large cement boulder a few feet away.

"Find anything?" she asked, leaning in to see what he was bent over.

He nodded, his fingers prodding at something in a large, realistic-looking lion's face. "I think so. Just one second..." Tugging hard, he stumbled back, just barely catching himself before he fell. He held out his left hand, and she smiled at the gold coin laying there.

"You found it!" Suppressing the urge to pick it up, Betsy turned back to the lion, sticking her finger into the now-empty eye socket. A folded piece of paper was jammed into the space and she carefully manipulated it enough to pull it free. "And this must be the clue. I wonder where we're going next?"

Ian stood beside the front window, looking out into the street. "You better find out fast," he said, striding quickly back across the room. "Looks like Derek found a way around the dresser. I just saw him poke his head out from between the Sultan's Palace and the Salon."

Betsy unfolded the note and read quickly, "Keep moseyin' for about one-thousand yards in the same direction. Look for Dusty. He's sporting a little bling these days."

Ian grabbed Betsy's hand and pulled her toward the back door. "There's only one thing that far away that makes sense," he said, checking out the alley before he tugged her out behind him. Jane didn't seem to be around, and he was glad - the last thing they needed was another confrontation right out in the open.

"The barn," Betsy said, pulling her fingers free. She tucked the note in her pocket. "Dusty's one of the horses, so we need to visit his stall next, right?"

Ian nodded, holding a finger to his lips as she caught up. "Not too loud. We don't know who he'll talk to next." He led her between the buildings behind Jane's, stopping at the corner to check the road before they darted across to the side of the mansion. Staying low, they ran thorough the trees to the narrow path that connected the dude ranch with the rest of the estate.

"Let's stay to the side," he said, leading the way through the thick forest brush to the left of the path. They jogged when they could, but it was still several minutes before the outlines of the bunkhouse and stables became visible. Ian crouched down behind a large bush near the edge of the clearing, looking through the branches to get his bearings.

"How do we get in without anyone seeing us?" he asked, glancing back at Betsy. Her eyes narrowed in confusion.

"Why does it matter? As long as Derek isn't here, it shouldn't matter who sees us, right? One of the cowboys might know where to look. Like Alex did."

"I just don't want to bring anyone else into this," he said. "We don't know what Derek will do if he gets desperate. I don't want anyone else getting hurt if we can help it."

"Oh, I think we can take care of ourselves, preacher." The deep drawl made Ian jump, and Betsy gasped. They turned to see worn boots, dusty jeans and the tip of a rifle barrel, luckily pointed at the ground rather than them.

"God, Chase - what the hell are you doing sneaking up on us like that?" Betsy rose to her feet and socked the cowboy in the shoulder. He just grinned at Ian, who managed to smile back. He fought to keep his expression from turning cold when Betsy threw her arms around Chase's shoulders, squeezing him in a big hug. Had she slept with this guy too? Ian hated himself for wondering.

Chase released Betsy, then offered a hand to Ian, pulling him up. "I was just coming back - was checking on some visitors who've had a couple horses out past the check-in time."

"Are they okay?" Betsy said, looking past him into the woods with a worried look on her face. Chance winked at Ian.

"Well, the horses looked kind of bored, but the guests seemed to be enjoying the warm spring, if you know what I mean."

Betsy smacked him in the arm again, though it looked more like a tap this time. "Chase McGowan.

You were not spying on a couple having...uh...making out."

He shrugged. "Gotta make sure my horses are okay," he said, balancing the rifle over his shoulder. "So what brings you two city slickers all the way out here?"

Ian started to speak, but Betsy beat him to it. "We're kind of on a little treasure hunt," she said, hooking her thumbs in her pockets. "We need to look in Dusty's stall, if that's okay with you."

He nodded. "Don't see why not. Mind if I tag along?"

Ian caught Betsy's hand, squeezing tight when she tried to pull away. "Actually," he said, noting Chase's gaze taking in their linked hands, "It's sort of a competition, so if you don't mind, we'll just go in alone. You understand." He stared into the other man's eyes, saw that he'd made his point.

Chase backed off, holding his free hand up. "Hey man, no problem. I see how it is. Just...don't leave a mess, okay?"

Betsy laughed, bumping his side as Chase wandered off. "Oh come on," she said once she looked at his face. "It was a joke, Ian. Funny. Now come on. Let's go see where a horse hides his gold."

Betsy tugged Ian toward the barn, her fingers still entwined with his. "If you didn't want Chase to think we were going to fool around, you shouldn't have been all macho-possessive," she teased, the hard set of his jaw somehow making her feel lighter. Her smile faded though when he didn't say anything, just followed her into the barn and pulled the doors shut behind them.

Then he grabbed her wrists and pushed her up against the wood wall, not hard enough to hurt but firmly just the same. Releasing her wrists, he braced his arms on either side of her, blocking her in.

Her blood raced with excitement as his intense stare captured her gaze and held it tight. This was a side of Ian she hadn't seen before, possessive and dominating. Leader of the pack, so to speak.

She wanted more.

"I didn't like it when you touched him," he said, that low, gruff tone vibrating through her entire body. "I liked it even less when he touched you."

She shrugged, peering up at him coyly through her eyelashes as she placed her hands on either side of his chest. "Well, it's not like we're an item now, is it Ian? I mean sure, we fooled around a bit, and kissed, but we haven't really talked about--"

He growled low in his throat just before he captured her lips with a punishing kiss.

Betsy's hands locked around his neck as his arms slid around her, crushing her against him. It felt like the world was swirling around her as his tongue took possession of her mouth, demanding the full surrender she was only too happy to give. His hands roamed her body, eliciting a gasp when cool fingers slid under her shirt to push her bra out of the way and cup her breast. He rolled her nipple between two fingers and she arched into him, begging shamelessly for more. She reached down and caressed him through his pants, her body aching to feel his thick length inside of her.

Then her jeans were unbuttoned, and she hurried to toe off her shoes and wriggle out of her pants as she struggled to release his zipper. His mouth never left her as he grabbed her ass and hoisted her up so she could wrap her legs around his hips. Finally he lowered her onto his waiting cock, sliding easily into her warm, moist heat. She whimpered with pleasure as he filled her completely, stretching her to a perfect fit.

Balanced between his chest and the wall, Betsy held him tight as his movements slowed. He kissed her neck, the hollow of her throat, her shoulder as she let her head fall back, opening herself completely to him. Then he drove deep, holding there until she raised her head to meet his warm gaze.

"Tell me you're mine, Betsy. Because I've been yours since we were kids, and I don't wanna fight it anymore."

Chapter Eight

Betsy smiled, running the fingers of one hand down the side of Ian's neck. "Isn't that what I've been telling you all along?" His cock twitched inside her, and she closed her eyes for a moment, reveling in the sensation. Opening them just part way, she clenched around him, rewarded with his sharp intake of breath. "Just promise me you won't forget we belong together again, okay? Now that I've got you, I'm not letting you go."

Ian nodded, then leaned in to capture her lips again, thrusting slow at first, and then building up steam. Betsy lost herself in the moment, closed her eyes and let her head fall back as he lay claim to her body. The pressure built rapidly, until she was practically screaming his name, but he did nothing to silence her like some men would have. His hand slid between their bodies and his thumb circled over her clit, one rotation all it took to make her world explode. Then he quickly lifted her off of him, and supported her with one arm while he pulled frantically on his cock with the other.

Still dazed, Betsy sank to her knees in the straw, not sure why he'd disengaged, but determined to make sure he got as good as he gave. Reaching for him, she ran her tongue over and around his smooth length before sucking him into her mouth. He grunted, trying to pull back but she looked up to meet his determined stare and winked.

Needing no more encouragement, his hips bucked against her face, and he thrust against the back of her throat, coming hard. She drank him down until he gently pulled her up and held her tight against his chest.

Her head against his heart, she listened to the beat even out as they breathed together. She started to draw back, not sure what to say but needing to see his expression when voices on the other side of the wall drew her attention.

"Get your clothes," Ian hissed, yanking his pants up over his hips. Betsy struggled into hers, not sure if they were right but knowing she didn't have time to care. She ran past Ian to the back of the barn, finding Dusty's stall and flinging herself into it, thankful that the horse wasn't there. Ian jogged in beside her, swinging the gate shut and crouching in the corner just as the main door to the building opened.

Rhythmic clopping signaled the entrance of horses, and Betsy hoped Dusty wasn't one of them. She let out a quiet sigh of relief when they stopped short of the last stall, and resigned herself to a long wait while the horses were taken care of. Letting her gaze roam over the comfortable space, she took in the sparse walls, her hope of finding the next coin fading with each stone. She wasn't sure what she'd expected, really - having tack in the stall seemed like it could be dangerous for the horse, but anything left here so long ago would surely have been cleaned out by now.

She jumped when long fingers intertwined with hers, then smiled when soft lips kissed her neck.

"Look up. The bottom of the hay rack," Ian whispered, his lips barely touching her ear. She tilted her head back to view the underside of a sturdy metal structure bolted into the wall above their heads.

She grinned at him, leaning in for another kiss.

Betsy reached up and tugged the clear plastic square free, careful not to make a sound. Ian held out his hand and she gave it to him, her heart racing as he popped the two halves apart. Wherever the next clue sent them would be the last stop on their half of the map, which meant Derek could be waiting at any of the hiding places after that. If he could decipher his half of the map without clues, anyway.

Ian handed her the coin, and she flipped it over once before putting it in her pocket with the others.

He unfolded a small piece of paper and his eyebrows drew together as he read it before passing that over too. Betsy stared down at the scrawled text, barely legible in the dim stall light, and suddenly she understood.

The handwriting was different.

Glancing up, she met Ian's gaze, silently confirming her fears. If this wasn't her friend's note, which meant someone had already found this hiding spot, and maybe even the others. Why had they left the coin though, or bothered to replace the original note? She looked again, studying the flow of the text for any clues. It wasn't anyone she knew well, which helped ease her discontent. Derek's handwriting was looser, more haphazard, so unless he had someone else write the note, it wasn't him. She breathed just a little easier, but not much. Someone out there had the rest of the clues, which means they had the location of the chest.

Along with everything in it.

Toward the front of the barn, a stall door clanged shut, and another just a few seconds later. The voices receded, fading the farther they got from the barn, and Ian motioned for her to stay put as he got to his knees.

Peeking through the metal bars of the stall door, he waited a few extra seconds, then got to his feet and leaned out to look down the corridor. Betsy was beginning to think he'd froze there until finally he came back, holding out a hand to help her up.

"Looks like we're clear," he said, his voice scratchy to start. He nodded toward the note. "Is that Derek, do you think?"

She shook her head and leaned over to brush off her pants. "Nope - his writing is completely different, thank goodness. I wonder how long this one's been there?"

"No way to tell," he said, rubbing a hand over his face. "But I do think we'd better hurry. We're nearly done with our half of the map. Who knows what Derek's managed to find with his. Can you tell where we're going next?

Betsy read the clue aloud. "The next coin belongs to the kingdom. Are you brave enough to slay the dragon for it?"

Ian shrugged. "A dragon is the least of our worries." He grabbed her hand, bending gallantly to kiss it. "Shall we retire to the castle, milady?"

She laughed. "Indeed, good sir. We'll hope the beast is in a good mood today."

Her hand nestled in his, Betsy followed Ian back toward the main compound of the ranch. The castle was situated in the southeast corner, and they would have to pass several of the larger buildings to gain access. Unfortunately, that made run-ins with the group Harley and Monica were entertaining - if you could call it that. As they skirted the edge of a meadow, she wondered how her brother and his new bride were doing. Hopefully better than it had been when she'd had to leave. If Harley would just quit being so stubborn and admit that he loved Monica...

She looked thoughtfully at Ian, then laughed, shaking her head. He glanced over at her, his brows drawn in confusion.

"What's so funny?"

She shook her head, and gave his hand a gentle squeeze. "You and Harley," she said, letting Ian help her over a fallen tree-trunk in their path. "You seem so different, and yet in a lot of ways you're so much the same. Both running from the thing you want most because you're convinced it's the one thing you can't have."

Ian stopped, pulling her in a wide circle that ended right in his arms. "And just how do you propose to know what it is that your brother wants most? Or me, for that matter?"

"Isn't it obvious?" She leaned back against him, reveling in the warmth of his body against hers and the way the sunshine felt on her face. "Harley never would have married Monica without feeling a strong bond with her, no matter what he says. He doesn't want to be alone - he wants the family we never really had."

Ian nodded, his ear against hers. "And me? What is it that I'm convinced I can never have?" His voice was so soft, yet so full of nuance that her knees almost buckled as his hot breath caressed her ear.

"Me," she whispered, not daring to break the stillness around them. "Or at least it was, until you finally
decided to give me a chance."

"How very touching. True love wins again and all
that jazz. Tell me, Ian - when's the wedding?"

Derek stepped onto the path in front of them, his
hands coming together in a slow golf-clap. Ian released his hold on her, but only long enough to gently
push her behind him.

"Next summer, if she'll have me. But I think the
more important questions are, how did you find us,
and when are you leaving?"

Derek shrugged. "I'm not leaving until I get my
money. And as for how I found you..." He pulled the
second half of the map out of his pocket and unfolded it. "That barn is the first thing on my map - easy
enough to decipher once I got a good look at the
compound and where things are. The castle has a very
nice view - pity you two won't be able to enjoy it from
where I plan to leave the two of you."

* * *

Ian held Betsy's hand as they entered what appeared to be a cellar at the back of the dungeon with
Derek close behind. Stepping carefully with only the
dim light of Derek's flashlight to illuminate the stairs,
Ian cringed every time he heard a creak caused by his
weight. When he was finally standing on bare earth,

he turned and grasped Betsy's waist, lifting her off the last few steps.

"Isn't that just frickin' adorable," Derek mocked as he joined them. Holding the flashlight beam straight ahead, he motioned with the gun. "Keep moving - take a left when you get to the wall."

Ian could feel Betsy open her mouth, and he squeezed her hand. The last thing they needed was to antagonize Derek. He pulled her behind him, moving quickly and following the stone wall as they turned. Just like all the other buildings in the compound, Harley and Betsy had done a spectacular job of making sure everything was as close to authentic as possible, right down to the sound of water dripping in the distance, and a damp chill that drifted through the passage.

"Turn right there," Derek said, and Ian turned, relieved that there were small barred windows around the edges of the main dungeon area. The small amount of light helped to make the space slightly less claustrophobic, though the chains and manacles bolted to the stone walls in several cells made his stomach twist.

"Get in that center cell. Away from the door."

Ian led Betsy into the small cube near the inner wall, three stone sides and floor-to-ceiling metal pipes on the fourth, with a large open door that Derek swung shut with a clang behind them.

"Now give me the last clue you found. I need to know where this half starts, and whoever was drawing this map can't draw for shit." He balanced the gun on one of the flat supports, and stuck the other hand through the bars, palm up. "Either cooperate, or it will be my pleasure to strip-search you, Bets. And I doubt even your preacher here can save you with a bullet in his chest." He frowned, looking thoughtfully at the floor before he raised his face again. "On second thought, maybe I'll shoot him in the leg. Then you can watch him bleed to death after I'm gone."

"Bastard." Betsy pulled the map out of her pocket, and handed it over before Ian could stop her. "You're not going to get away with this, you know. Even if you do manage to figure out all the clues, it will be too late."

Derek backed away from the cell, his laughter echoing through the chamber. "I always like that about you," he said, stuffing the gun in his waistband and opening up the paper. "Feisty. When I'm done, I'll be back for you. Then you can see what it's like to be taken captive by a real pirate after he's looted the ship. Arrrg." He snapped his teeth at her, then turned on his heel and marched out of the dungeon, muttering to himself as he went.

"I think he's actually gone insane this time," Betsy commented, shaking her head. "I have no idea what I ever saw in that guy." She reached for one end of a wooden bench along the far wall, motioning for Ian to help.

He picked up the other end and followed her to the southwest corner of the cell, where she set her end down, and he settled his perpendicular to the wall. "What are we doing?"

She glanced over her shoulder, looking as far outside of the bars as she could. "Getting out of here," she whispered, then pointed up. Ian tipped his head back, and grinned.

"You knew that was there all along. Smart girl."

She shrugged. "I insisted in designing them that way when we first started. I figured with the real locks, it would be too easy to get stuck accidentally, so all of the cells have an escape hatch at the top. You can come back down here, or you can take one of a few hidden passageways to other parts of the castle. Like the tower room, where he's going now." She stood on the bench, stretching to pull the square wooden hatch down.

Ian stepped up beside her, putting his hands on her waist so he could lift her up. "Is that where we're going? That's where the next clue leads, right?"

She shook her head and winked. "That's right, but that's not where we're going. Because while we were walking here, I figured it out. I know where the treasure is, so we're going there instead."

Chapter Nine

Betsy waited for Ian to join her in the narrow passage, then they closed the hatch, careful not to make any noise. A small amount of light from tall, narrow slats at either end of the stone hallway provided just enough light to move safely over the other hatches.

"This way," she said, leading him toward the back of the castle and passing the first opening, then the second. "We'll go out the back. He's less likely to see us that way from the tower." She led the way down a narrow stairway barely wide enough for one person, sliding her hand along the wall until she found the switch to activate the electric torches on the walls.

"Where are we going?" Ian asked from behind, his voice echoing through the tunnel. Betsy stopped to look back, holding a finger to her lips and smiling when he mouthed "Sorry."

"I'll let you know as soon as we get out of here, okay?"

He nodded, and she turned, taking the last few steps down and waiting again at the bottom. He started to reach around her for the door, and she shook her head.

"That leads straight into the back salon - we'll be exposed. It will be better to go through the kitchen. This way." She pointed to her left, where a short hall led to a blank wall. It was all she could do not to chuckle at Ian's confusion when he looked back at her. Moving past him, she winked, and then walked up to the wall, running her fingers down each side of the stone, and then pressed in with both fists about half-way down. A quiet click, and the wall pivoted in the middle, revealing a long, ancient-looking table and a massive open stone fireplace beyond. Glancing back with a grin, she motioned for Ian to join her, then slid through the opening to the other room.

The secret door back in place, Betsy grabbed Ian's hand and pulled him past the modern appliances styled to fit in with the decor, wishing they had time to play. Taking only a second to look through the back window, she tugged him out into the lean-to and then stopped at the last door between them and freedom.

"We need to get across the road to Ecstasy," she said, keeping her voice low, and leaning close. "I don't know why I didn't think of it before, but it makes complete sense. Hidden treasure, map, X marks the spot...and when she was here, Ecstasy was just being constructed, so it would have been easy to hide something at the site. But we should hurry--"

Ian held up a hand, looking confused. "So you think that Ecstasy equals the proverbial X? Are you sure? That seems a little too easy after all of this running around."

She nodded. "The point was never to make it hard, remember? My friend was just having fun. We need to hurry though. If Derek hasn't figured it out already, he will soon. The tower has a great view of all the buildings on this side of the compound, and Ecstasy is marked with a big, bold X that covers the roof. It was Harley's idea to mark the compound for anyone flying over, and it fit with the theme, you know?"

"Any idea where the chest will be when we get there?" Ian opened the door and stepped outside, staying close to the building. He looked up, and Betsy followed his gaze, satisfied that they weren't visible from the upper levels of the castle.

"My guess is somewhere in the attic," she said, following him south to the far corner of the building. "Right under the X."

Ian shook his head. "No way it could be that easy," he said, leaning out to look around the corner of the building. Betsy peeked around him, seeing nothing but grass between them and the road.

"We were drinking, remember? Personally, I think hiding what amounts to a small treasure under the biggest X you can find is a brilliant idea. It's so obvious and corny that no one would ever guess." She leaned back against the building and pushed her hands into her pockets to think.

"We need a distraction," he said, the words echoing her own thoughts. "I'm not sure what though. We don't want to draw too much attention, but we need enough to draw Derek's focus somewhere else long enough for us to get across the street."

Betsy nodded, quickly considering several ideas and just as quickly tossing them out. Considering they didn't want to involve anyone else, only one choice remained.

"We'll split up," she said, holding a hand up when Ian looked like he would protest. "He'll see you going one way with a piece of paper in your hand, and me going the other way. He'll have to choose which one of us to follow."

"He'll follow you." Ian took her hands and looked down into her eyes. "But you already thought of that, didn't you?"

"Yes." She looked up at him, willing him to go along with it. "Derek will follow me, and you can get the treasure. We'll meet back here in a couple of hours. In the tower room. It won't occur to him that we'd come here."

Ian quirked an eyebrow at her. "What about the secret stashed with your coins? I thought you didn't want anyone touching that."

Betsy looked past his shoulder, unable to look him in the eye. "If you and I...well...if we're going to be together, you should know what's there. Just make sure Derek doesn't get it, and I'll tell you everything. I promise."

"Hey," he said, sliding a hand along her cheek and turning her face to his. His expression was serious, but kind, and she relaxed against the warmth from his body. "Whatever it is, we'll deal with it together. I promise."

"I hope so," she said, sliding out of his grasp. "We should go now. He's probably already seen the mark...we need to keep him away." She glanced up at Ian, ignoring the concern on his face. "I'll lead him to the main building, and circle back through the guest rooms to lose him. We'll meet back here in...forty-five minutes?"

He nodded, but put a hand on her arm to stop her when she turned away. "What if you can't lose him? I don't like this, Betsy. We should call someone in to help."

"There isn't time." She shook off his hand and smiled. "Don't you worry about me. Just get that file, and keep it safe. That's all that matters now."

She turned and ran for the street, not daring to look back even though she felt the heat of his stare.

Even if Derek did catch her, it didn't matter as long as Ian kept the file safe.

Betsy didn't look back as she ran, taking cover briefly around the corner of a building, then sprinting for the next before stopping again. The third time she stopped behind a thick tree, and cautiously peeked around the other side to make sure he was following. At first, she didn't see anything, but then a small flutter of movement across the road caught her eye.

Frowning, she squinted in an attempt to make out details as a figure came around the corner of Ecstasy. The sun was in just the exact spot to cast the figure in shadow, and she closed her eyes, willing them to somehow see through the black as she blinked them open again. The figure walked toward where she was hiding and she knew she'd have to move soon, no matter who the man was. But she could see well enough to spot the thick manila envelope in his hands, and her pulse raced as she hoped against hope it was Ian approaching. But why was he just strolling out in the open like that?

"You can come out now, Darlin'," Derek yelled, confirming her worst fears. "I got the papers I wanted and it looks like I don't need your signature to get into those accounts after all. You can keep the coins that I left up there - something to remember me and little Ainsley by. Or maybe you'd rather just forget you had a daughter...is that why you gave her up? Or was it to keep her from me? Too late, 'cause I already knew."

Betsy moved from behind the tree, her nemesis holding up Ainsley's adoption papers and a note with her adoptive parents' address with it. She tried to look normal, like it wasn't a big deal, but it was. If Derek got his hands on their little girl, she'd have no chance at a normal life - and she'd learn the truth about her real father. Betsy was determined not to let that happen, at any cost.

"You stay away from her, Derek. She has a good life - a normal life, and I won't let you mess that up for her. Name your price - anything. Just promise me you'll leave her alone."

Over Derek's shoulder, Betsy saw Ian sneaking closer. Maybe if she could keep Derek distracted...

"Who told you, anyway? You weren't supposed to know about...that."

He laughed, as if it was the stupidest thing he'd ever heard. "You forget, my dear - I have eyes everywhere. You really think I'd let you break up with me and not have you watched? I've known every move you made since I was locked up, sometimes before you made it. You can't hide from me, Betsy, and as for my price..." he looked her up and down, the gleam in his eye making her want to throw up. "There's only one other thing I want more than our daughter, Betsy. One way you can keep me from taking her back from those nice people."

She swallowed hard, not seeing Ian anymore. She already knew the answer, but she had to ask anyway, just to keep him talking for a little while longer.

"What's that, Derek? What do you want?"

He grinned. "You, of course. I want you."

* * *

Ian knew he had to move quickly or Betsy might not make it out of this. He knew she'd never let Derek take her alive. Grabbing a shovel out of the shed he'd stepped behind, Ian steeled himself for what he had to do. Breathing in deep, he rushed toward Derek and raised the makeshift weapon to strike.

Then something hit the back of his left arm, hard. The momentum spun him around and stole his balance, sending him crashing to the ground. Landing hard, his ribs connected solidly with the wooden handle, and a sickening crunch vibrated up through his ears. The world around him ceased to exist, the pain engulfing his entire being stronger than anything he'd ever felt before. Cold numbness followed quickly, and the far off sound of someone screaming was the last thing he heard before everything went black.

* * *

A constant annoying ache in his ribs warred with the rhythmic throbbing in his upper arm when Ian came to. Opening his eyes, he tried to sit up, the resulting stab of pain in his torso causing him to fall back with a moan. Nearby, a man chuckled.

"Nothing better to keep someone in line than his own nervous system," an unfamiliar voice commented. "You won't be moving again for awhile, so you might as well try to relax as much as you can."

Ian took a shallow breath - the only kind that didn't cause his ribcage to rebel. "Who are you, and where am I?" He glanced in the general direction of the voice, but it was too dark to make out anything more than a general profile.

The man chuckled again. "You're in bed, and my job is to see that you stay there. That's all you need to know, preacher-man."

"You work for Derek," Ian said, closing his eyes as another wave of pain moved under his skin. "Where's Betsy? Is she okay?"

"She's alive, if that's what you mean. She and the boss had some business to take care of."

Forcing his eyes open again, Ian tried to orient himself in the room. There was a window to his right that provided a minimal amount of light from the moon, so it was obviously night. Various shapes around the room seemed to be furniture - a dresser and chairs, maybe, but it all seemed foreign. He remembered rushing Derek with the shovel, then falling...

"You knocked me over." He looked at the man's profile again, this time noticing the shape of a gun held casually across one thigh.

"Bullet did that. If my aim was better, we wouldn't be having this conversation. I'm a little out of practice, I'm afraid."

Ian frowned. "So why not just finish me off then?"

His guard shrugged. "Derek seems to think his woman will cooperate better if she thinks there's hope you'll make it through. Considering how fast she agreed to go with him when we offered to patch you up, I'm inclined to agree."

Chapter Ten

Betsy drove as slowly as she dared on the interstate, the butt of Derek's gun bumping against her neck every so often. She'd been to the house before, a couple times - just to watch, of course. It had been too painful to visit often, knowing she could never give her daughter the kind of normal life that her adoptive parents gave her. The thought of Derek ripping that all away...

"Why?" she asked, swallowing around the lump in her throat. "Why would you do this to her? You have me. Why can't you just leave her alone, let her be happy and lead a normal life?"

The cold metal pressed purposefully into her skin. "Are you saying I can't give our daughter a normal life? You think I can't make her happy?"

She glanced at him in the rear view mirror, his narrowed eyes meeting hers. "Of course...of course you could," she stuttered, not meaning a word of it. Knowing she didn't dare argue further, she clamped her lips shut. If he shot her, Ainsley didn't have a chance.

After a few seconds, the barrel eased into a more relaxed position.

"Good girl," he said, letting out a husky laugh. "No one likes a whiner. As for why I want our daughter to live with us, that's simple. If she's around, you'll behave. I suspect you'll do just about anything for her."

Betsy frowned. "I thought that's why you agreed to help Ian," she said, dread thickening in her chest. "What happens to him after we pick up Ainsley?"

Derek laughed again, and she checked the mirror as he relaxed into the seat. "You didn't think he was coming to live with us, did you? And I can't really just let him go. What did you think would happen, Bets? You just bought him a few more hours, is all."

She stared out the windshield, biting back tears. If they reached Ainsley, Ian was dead. If they didn't, both she and Ian were dead, and Derek would get Ainsley anyway. The exit she needed to take was coming up quickly, it occurred to her that there was one other option. Ian may still not survive, but her little girl would be safe.

Scanning the landscape, she cursed the flat Nevada desert on either side. Careful to keep her expression neutral, she wished she'd paid better attention to the terrain before. Her palms too warm against the wheel, she tightened her grip as the road finally started sloping up. This hill wasn't tall enough, but as she sifted through the images in her mind, she remembered a steep climb just before the exit.

And a steep drop-off just on the other side that would work nicely.

Cresting the apex of the smaller slope, she saw her target approaching quickly. Easing down on the accelerator, she hit the next slope hard and fast, feeling the bite of metal against her neck again.

"Slow down," Derek commanded. "You need to take this exit."

Betsy shook her head. If he shot her now, he'd never survive the resulting crash, which suited her just fine. "I'm not taking the exit."

The safety clicked off as she pressed the pedal to the floor. "You are going to die if you don't take that damn exit right now."

"You're right," she said as they blew by the off ramp, satisfied to see fear in his eyes as she quickly checked the mirror. "I am going to die. And so are you."

Then she yanked the wheel to the right, sending the car through the guardrail with a horrible squealing noise as metal scraped against metal. For a long moment, it felt like time stopped and Betsy felt like the car hung in mid-air. Then the brush-covered hillside rose up to meet them, and the scene outside the front window was a blur of gold, green and gray as the car rolled down the slope. When it stopped, the final impact was too much, and everything went dark.

* * *

An irritating buzzing sound kept intruding on Betsy's sleep. She reached out to turn off the alarm, but something sharp pricked the palm of her hand and she jerked it back in pain. Her head felt weird as she tried to stretch with little success. Opening her eyes, she gasped at Derek's bloody face barely a foot away. Cold tremors started under her skin as she remembered why she was hanging upside down by her seat belt in the car. Derek hadn't been so lucky, from the looks of it.

Good.

The buzzing started again, and she tilted her head back to the cell phone resting on what had been the roof of the cab just below her. It was Derek's, and she carefully picked it up, mindful of the glass she'd cut herself on seconds before. There was an incoming text message, and she read it.

"Haven't heard from you - are we still on schedule? I'll check in again at four. If I don't talk to you then, I know what to do. "

Betsy set the phone down carefully, and then reached for the seat belt. She had to get out of there -

already she could hear sirens in the distance, and she couldn't risk being taken to the hospital before she made sure her little girl was safe. Then she had to find Ian.

The clasp wouldn't budge, no matter how hard she pulled. Leaning back down, she grabbed a sharp piece of glass and sawed at the fabric until it was barely connected. Leaning back with one hand, she braced herself as well as she could, and then tugged the last bit of the strap apart.

Gravity took over, and she slipped out of the seat, landing on her shoulders. After a few minutes of careful maneuvering and more cuts, she managed to crawl out the window to safety. Her head spun as she sat up, and she nearly blacked out as the blood reversed course. Voices carried down to her from above, but looking up all she could see was the thick canopy of tall trees, minus some limbs they'd brought down with the car.

She stood carefully, bracing herself on a boulder for support. After a few quick checks to make sure her joints all worked, she jogged off into the woods, stopping only briefly to reply to the text with one of her own.

"Slight delay. Do nothing until you hear from me."

Betsy kept moving for the next half-hour, stopping on top of a small rise to get her bearings. Finding a cell signal, she tried to call her brother, but there was no answer. Tapping into the GPS program and was relieved to realize that the city was just a couple miles from her position. Looking out that direction, she sighed. The large hill she'd run the car off of was just part of a range, from the looks of it. The only way to get back to the other side was to go back to the interstate and around, or to climb directly over. She could see the highway off to her right, but to get there would make the trip twice as long. Either way, she needed water, and the sun was starting to go down, which meant colder temperatures than she was dressed for.

Swiping at frustrated tears, she leaned against a tree knowing that if she sat down she might not get back up. As she looked across the valley, she tried to think of who she could call, but aside from Harley and Monica, there really wasn't anyone else who would care enough to come get her except Ian. Just the thought of him being held by Derek's men brought fresh tears to her eyes.

Out of the corner of her eye, she saw something glint in the sun at the base of the hill, and she forced herself to move for a better vantage point. As she walked out of the trees and peered around a large boulder, a slow smile spread across her lips.

* * *

Betsy scrambled down the slope, nearly losing her footing several times in her haste. She approached the two newer-looking trucks cautiously, wondering just how far away the owners were. Seeing no one, she opened the driver's side door of the closest vehicle as quietly as she could, only wide enough to allow her to slide under the wheel. Laying across the seat, she pulled the wires from the ignition down, took a breath, and tapped them together a few times, hoping the truck had fuel. As the engine roared to life, she sat up and threw the transmission into drive, stepping on the gas as two half-dressed teens came around the corner of the hill, yelling and waving their arms.

Glancing in the rear view mirror as she headed towards the highway, she saw one of the kids put a phone to his ear. She didn't have much time, and when she reached the ramp to get on the interstate, she hesitated. If she went toward the city, she'd have to pass the accident, and all the law enforcement people who were probably still there. By now, dispatch had probably already radioed the truck description out. Damn cell phones.

Derek was dead though, or close to it - either way, he wouldn't be visiting their daughter anytime soon. And if she went back to the ranch, there was a chance she might be able to find Ian before

The phone in her pocket buzzed, and she dug it out, her heart in her throat as she read the text on the screen.

"Feds are here. Gotta move. Meet at location B."

Betsy swore. Cranking the wheel to the south, she got on the highway headed back toward the ranch. There was a turnoff a few miles further, and if she could reach that, she could disappear on the back roads for the remainder of the drive. Grabbing the phone off the seat, she punched in a number she'd memorized years ago, but had never used.

"Hello?" A woman's voice came on the line, and thankfully she sounded like an adult. Betsy took a breath.

"One of your children might be in danger. If you see anyone suspicious hanging around outside, call the police right away. It's important."

She hung up before any questions could be asked, and tossed the phone back on the seat, flicking away a stray tear. It was all she could do right now, but it felt like too little. Hopefully it wouldn't be too late.

Around the next bend, she saw the exit coming up and breathed a sigh of relief. Veering off the interstate, she turned onto an empty two-lane frontage road and floored it, thinking of all the places on the ranch someone could hide out. Derek had mentioned awhile back that he'd been staying out there, so obviously he'd found a spot. Unfortunately, it was probably in the cave-system below, considering he'd managed to stay hidden so long. She shivered at the thought of going back down there, but it was the only logical choice, especially if there were federal agents on the ranch.

Wondering briefly why that would be, she frowned. Was Harley in some sort of trouble? Maybe that's why he hadn't answered.

She turned onto an old mining road just inside the ranch boundary and stopped the truck in a clearing about twenty feet in. She'd have to move it later, but for now, it should be fine. Climbing out, she ran a few feet into the trees until she found the vine-covered wooden door, and used the spare key hidden under a log to unlock it. Replacing the key, she stepped over the threshold and found the flashlight on the floor to her right before locking the door behind her.

Steeling herself with a long sigh, she pointed the flashlight ahead and began her descent back into the tunnel system.

* * *

Ian woke to brighter light coming in through translucent white curtains. His throat was dry and he rolled to his side, wincing at the dull ache that banded his torso. Remembering his captor, he looked toward the chair in the corner, but it was empty. A quick glance around the room told him he was alone, which suited him fine. Judging from the simple furnishings, he was in one of the guest rooms of the mansion - rooms that weren't rented out to just anyone. Normally reserved for people with a lot more money than

Derek had, Ian assumed no one knew the room was occupied.

He fought his way to a sitting position, barely succeeding at holding in a groan. He'd only been in these upper suites once before, but he remembered that each room had it's own restroom, and after carefully rising to his feet, he shuffled in the direction it should be. Thankful he remembered correctly, he relieved himself and then got a drink of water, splashing some over his face while he was at it.

A clock on the counter read four in the afternoon, and he frowned. If memory served, that meant he'd been there a whole day. But where was Betsy?

A click outside the bathroom door signified the return of his captor. Ian looked around the small room, trying to find something, anything he could use as a weapon. Settling on the towel bar, he dropped the towel on the floor and yanked up, then out to break it free from its anchor. He turned just as the bathroom door burst open.

He brought the rod up hard underneath the man's wrists, catching him by surprise and knocking the gun into the air. The weapon landed with a loud crash in the bathtub behind him, but aside from being grateful it didn't go off, Ian didn't have time to grab it. Driven by pure adrenaline, he raised the bar with both hands and brought it down in the other man's right thigh, earning a squeal of pain and some room as the man stumbled back. Ian raised the metal again, intending to strike in the center of the chest.

In that instant, he was aware of two things: The man was reaching for another gun strapped to his ankle, and Ian didn't want to kill anyone.

The man raised the gun, his finger on the trigger.

Ian brought the bar down hard, piercing the man's belly. Blood splashed up over Ian's hands as the man cried out, the gun dropping from his fingers as he passed out. Ian yanked the bar back out and tossed it aside, gathering the two guns and stepping over the dying guard. His mind felt strangely numb, as though he was seeing everything play out in slow motion. Knowing the man would die but unable to watch, he closed the bathroom door and hobbled across the room, fresh stripes of pain twisting his ribs and head.

"God forgive me," he whispered, shoving the guns under the pillow and laying back on the bed. He needed to rest, just for a minute. Then he'd find his way out.

A minute later, he was asleep.

Chapter Eleven

Exhausted, Betsy slid down the cool dirt wall and aimed the flashlight beam on a map. It felt like she'd been walking for hours, but there was no sign of Ian or even anyone suspicious that might lead her to him. The tunnels beneath the ranch were cold and eerily quiet, the lack of sound and companionship getting to her more than anything else. If Ian was down here, there was no way she'd find him by herself. She needed help.

If she'd followed the landmarks correctly, which she wasn't at all sure of, the tunnel that began directly in front of her should lead to the access door under the mansion. Exhaling long and slow, she forced herself to get up and started down the dark passageway. Swinging the light from side to side, she moved as quickly as she dared, trying to be quiet. Then she saw it - a sliver of brightness piercing the dark several feet ahead.

Panic was her first reaction, because down here, there shouldn't be any open doors or light penetrating. Either someone had entered or left the tunnels there recently, or a door had been left open - something no one who knew about them would dare to do. Her heart beating fast, Betsy switched off the light and hugged the wall, inching slowly closer. By the time she was near enough to peer around the corner, her mouth was so dry and her pulse so quick she could barely swallow.

Half-expecting a large hand to reach out for her, she leaned against the corner and twisted around until she could see. Her eyes widened as she took in the jagged edges of rock that framed a small, crudely shaped opening. There was no door, but on the other side of the opening she could swear she saw...

Shower tile?

Her instincts told her the area was empty, and she moved toward the opening, flashlight held ready as a weapon. Stopping just outside the portal she waited, listening for any sound at all before stepping through into a large shower area she recognized as her brother's.

"What on earth has he been up to?" she mused softly, making her way to the bathroom door. She pressed her ear against it, listening for several seconds before pulling it open.

The place felt deserted, and her panic subsided as she went through the living room and got a glass of water in the kitchen. Remembering the cell phone, she tried to call Harley again, but he still didn't answer. Gulping down more fluid, she brought up the text messages Derek's goon had sent her earlier, and pressed the button to reply.

"I'm here - where are you?" she typed in, hoping he'd take the bait. Expecting a quick reply, she stared at the screen for several minutes, sipping water as a clock ticked somewhere in the next room.

The minute she gave up and laid the phone on the counter, it buzzed. Snatching it up, she read the words on the screen with a grin.

"Upstairs, mansion. Hurry."

Ian set the phone on a low table near the door, glad it had woke him up in time to get the text from Derek. Looking around for a weapon, he settled on the thick wooden dowel that served as a closet rod. He considered getting one of the guns, but he didn't want to risk killing Derek before he found out where Betsy was. With any luck, she was here at the ranch too, but it didn't matter. He'd do whatever he had to do to get her back, no matter where Derek had stashed her.

The floor creaked in the hall, and Ian sucked in a breath. There was a short hall between the door and the main part of the room, and he braced his back against the wall on one side of the opening. The door handle jiggled, and he wondered for a minute if he'd locked it, but then a beam of light penetrated the darkness as the door swung open. He waited, his heart thudding in his chest as he held the dowel ready to swing like a bat.

A taller, thinner figure stepped into the room, and even as he started to swing, he realized it wasn't - couldn't be - Derek standing just two feet away. There was definitely something familiar about the person though, and he dropped the dowel mid-swing as he recognized her scent.

"Betsy?"

She turned just as he stepped forward, and a sharp zing of pain sliced through his stomach like a giant paper cut.

"Oh my god - Ian!" She pulled her arm back, tossing the knife she'd been holding on the bed as he fell against the wall and slid down. His stomach felt like it was on fire as she turned on a light, then knelt beside him on the floor.

"I was expecting one of Derek's men, or more," she explained pulling at the bandages already wrapped around his middle. "I had no idea - why didn't you say something when I came in?"

Ian looked down as she finally tore the cotton strips, wincing as the pressure on his ribs released.

"I was expecting Derek," he said, watching her probe at the wound. "Is it deep? It doesn't feel deep..." He closed his eyes, focusing on his stomach, but the pain seemed localized in his skin. When he opened his eyes, he found Betsy looking at him with a strange clarity in her eyes. It was beautiful and mesmerizing all at once, with a hint of sadness as well.

"It's not deep, thank goodness," she said finally, breaking eye contact to glance around the room. "I can sew it up if we have any supplies.

Ian pointed toward the bed. "All the stuff they used on me is in that table. Maybe there's something there." He watched her rifle through a plain cardboard box before she came back with a small white first aid kit.

"I don't think they intended for you to survive," she said, opening the kit and dumping the contents on the floor. "There's nothing here except band aids and a lot of gauze and wipes. I guess I could pull it together with band aids for now.

Ian chuckled. "Don't sound so excited." He watched as she worked, doing his best to stay still, though his ribs were throbbing. When she finished, she leaned back, but he caught her wrist and pulled her off balance so she had no choice but to sit next to him, under the curve of his arm.

She looked up at him, that mesmerizing look back, and he couldn't help himself.

"Come here," he whispered, pulling his arm tighter and her head closer at the same time. Her eyes drifted shut, and he pressed his lips to hers, reveling in the tiny sigh she gave before opening to him completely.

* * *

In the back of her mind, Betsy knew she should pull away. Ian was hurt, and she didn't want to make anything worse - especially since she was responsible for one of his injuries. But when he pulled her close and his lips touched hers, she was powerless to resist the indulgence.

He nibbled gently at her lips, teasing with a flick of the tongue as she opened for him, her body molding to his side as his grip tightened. She marveled at how perfectly they fit, how wonderful it felt to be snuggled up close to this man. She'd die a happy woman if she never moved again.

A loud, harsh noise filled the room, and Ian groaned even as he pulled away. Betsy blinked her eyes, confused and annoyed by the interruption as she watched Ian pull a cell phone out of his pocket.

"I took this off the guy guarding me," he said, holding up the phone before he checked the small screen. "It's the one you sent that text to."

Betsy nodded, leaning in to look at the screen as well. "Another text?"

Ian nodded. "Derek wants to know if I'm still alive."

"That's not possible," she said, pulling back and shaking her head. "When I left him, Derek was hanging upside down bloody and unconscious at the bottom of a ravine. There's no way he could have survived it. No way."

"Did you check his pulse?"

Betsy tried to remember. Had she? She'd been so worried about getting out of there before the emergency crews arrived...and he'd looked pretty bad. She'd grabbed his phone and ran.

"I don't think so, now that you ask. I just had to get out of there. Away from him. And I knew that if the emergency crews caught me there, I'd be hauled off to the hospital or jail and I wouldn't be able to find you or check on...what is it?"

Ian's jaw tightened, and something in her gut told her this wasn't over yet. He turned the phone so she could easily read the entire screen.

"Kill the preacher. Meet at cabin 1 hour. D."

She sat up, regretting the loss of his warmth. "If he's still alive, Ainsley is still in danger. We need to find that cabin."

Ian frowned. "Who's Ainsley? And why is she in danger?"

Betsy froze. She'd forgotten he didn't know. Looking down at her hands, she tried to ignore the panic that made her hands shake. Would he think less of her for giving up her own daughter? Would he understand why she'd had no choice? The clock on the wall ticked away precious seconds she knew they couldn't afford.

"Ainsley is my daughter," she said, rising to pace in front of him. "It's a long story, but the short version is, I gave her up for adoption so Derek couldn't get to her. He found out, and now he wants her back. The adoption details were--"

"With the treasure." Ian nodded. "You should have told me. I thought we were better friends than that."

"I'm sorry. I'm not used to trusting people. But none of that matters now. Can't we talk about this later? What if he already has her?" She reached down to help Ian off the floor. "I called her adoptive parents, but I couldn't say much. We have to go now. What if we're too late? I should have destroyed those papers." She turned toward the door, her flight stopped only by Ian's firm grip on her arm.

"Hang on," he said, his hold unrelenting. "Running off in a panic isn't going to help. Call your daughter's family - there's a phone on the nightstand there - and tell them to get to safety. I'll see if maybe this goon was stupid enough to put the cabin's location in the GPS of this cell. Then we can decide where to go first."

Adrenaline flooding her system, Betsy balked at the wait, but she knew he was right. Calm and logical, as always. Reluctantly she nodded and then went to the phone, dialing the number as she watched Ian start searching through the cell phone programs.

After six unanswered rings, she hung up. "No one's answering, Ian. I don't know..."

He held up the cell phone for her to see. "The last destination this guy went to before the ranch seems to be out in the middle of nowhere. I bet that's where the cabin is. Lucky for us, he left the coordinates in his address book." He turned off the phone and shoved it in his pocket, then gave her a sympathetic look. "I know you want to go check on Ainsley, but I really think we should meet Derek at the cabin first. If he's got her, going to the house won't make any dif-ference, and he'll probably bring her with him to meet us. If he doesn't have her, they're not home which will make them harder to find. Win-win."

She nodded, knowing it made the most sense. "You're right. Let's go. He took me in his car, so mine should still be in the lot. We can take that." Leading the way to the hall, she stopped abruptly, frowning.

"You really should stay here. You're hurt. Let me call Harley or someone else to go. Heck, we should call the police so they can meet us there."

"I'm going with you," Ian said, his tone firm. "And I don't think we should call just yet. If I'm wrong, and we have the wrong place, it will just go badly for us. We can call when we're sure he's there." He brushed past her, leading the way to the stairs with one arm wrapped around his middle. "Any idea where Harley might have a spare weapon stashed?"

She nodded, hurrying to follow him. "Dad's collection is in the parlor. We can get whatever we need there." She led the way to the back of the mansion, peeking through the old lace curtains before opening the French doors. Punching in the combination, she opened the glass case and let Ian choose a handgun, then got a smaller model for herself. Locking the cabinet, she found ammunition, and then followed Ian out the back.

They kept to the trees, and Betsy was impressed at the speed Ian was able to maintain. Ten minutes later, they were headed down the highway. She desperately hoped Derek had gone directly to the cabin, instead of chasing Ainsley.

* * *

The cabin was larger than Betsy had envisioned, more like a ranch home built out of logs. Looking for other vehicles, she turned onto the gravel road and found a place to park behind some tall bushes near the end of the drive.

"I don't see any other cars near the house," she said as she turned off the engine. Glancing over at Ian, she noted how stiffly he held himself in the seat. "You must be in a lot of pain. We should have found some painkillers before we left the ranch."

He shook his head, checking his gun before he pushed the car door open. "Thanks, but I don't need a foggy brain for this. A little pain sharpens the senses, right?" He grinned, that know-it-all smirk he'd developed as a kid. It showed his bad-boy side, and Betsy had always been a sucker for that.

"Fine," she said, getting out of the car and checking her own weapon. "How do you want to do this, Rambo?"

He peered around the bushes, his expression serious. "He's expecting his guard, if he's in there, but I'm pretty certain he won't shoot you. Are you up for the straightforward approach? You can knock on the front door, and I'll head around the back. If you can keep him busy, I can flank him."

Betsy nodded. "What if he has my daughter?"

Ian turned, running his fingers down one side of her face. "Do what you have to do to keep her safe. I'll jump in as soon as I can."

She swallowed around the sudden lump in her throat. "Okay. And Ian?"

"Yeah."

"Be careful." She reached for him, pressing her lips to his in a quick kiss. Then she looked into his eyes for a long moment, and started walking toward the house.

When she reached the porch, she knocked on the front door. Gun aimed at the solid wood, she waited, her pulse racing when the knob finally turned.

The door swung open slowly, and she frowned when no one appeared behind it. Then finally, a small face peered out around the edge, much lower than she'd expected to see a face.

"Who are you?" she asked, frantically trying to come up with a way of getting the child out before Derek knew she was gone. Did he really think he could just kidnap any kid and pass her off as theirs? Or had he really grabbed the wrong one? Either way, she'd make sure he went back to prison - this time for good.

The little girl didn't answer. She just stared at the gun in Betsy's hands, frozen in place.

"Are you alone? You can just nod your head, sweetheart - yes or no." She waited for what felt like hours before the child finally nodded yes. Then the small eyes both glanced behind the door, and Betsy tightened her grip. She held one finger to her lips and started moving toward the door, slowly, staying low.

"Betsy? I saw you walking across the yard. You've kept us waiting long enough, don't you think?"

Derek sounded jovial, like he had early in their relationship when he'd downed a bottle of Jack. She hadn't planned on him being drunk. That made him far less predictable, and far more dangerous.

"How about a trade, Derek?" She stood up, letting the gun hang limp from her right hand as she stretched her arms wide in surrender. "You let her go, you get me. Simple and easy."

He laughed, the sound chilling her to her core. "You wish, sweetheart. I saw your preacher-man go around back. Think I heard one of my boys take care of him a few seconds ago, so you're on your own. If you don't want to see these little brains splattered across the floor, you'd better drop that gun on the porch and get your sweet ass in here - now."

Chapter Twelve

Unable to see anything but the girl, Betsy knew she had no choice but to give in to Derek's demand. Slowly she lowered the gun to the porch and kicked it toward the steps. His voice had come from behind the door, and she deliberately stepped over the threshold in a way that put her between him and the girl. As expected, he stood waiting, a look of triumph in his eyes as he pushed the door shut and reached around her to flip the deadbolt into place.

"Now," he said, motioning for her to move farther into the room. "Why don't we sit down and have a chat. I wasn't expecting you so soon, but I presume the guard I left with the preacher is dead."

Holding a hand out to the little girl, Betsy clasped the small fingers and led her to the couch, sitting down and patting the space between her and the plush sofa arm.

"He's dead," Betsy confirmed as Derek took the chair opposite them. "Where's my daughter?" She knew she needed to stay calm, and tried to focus on her breathing. She couldn't do anything to put the girl in danger. There was a kitchen behind them, and a hallway just beside that she assumed led to the back of the house. A small spiral staircase rose up in the corner behind Derek - access to a loft, perhaps?

"*Our* daughter is...unable to join us at the moment," Derek said. "She'll be along shortly though, don't you worry. In the meantime, we have some business to discuss."

"You've got a captive audience now. What do you want from me, Derek?" She wished he'd just come out and tell her, once and for all, so they could all get on with their lives. "If it's money you want, you could have taken the gold at the ranch. And you'll never have me or Ainsley - not while there's a breath left in my body."

He smiled. "Ah, but you're here now, so I do have you now don't I?"

Betsy shook her head. "You don't even know what you want, do you? Do you even have an end game here? What's it all for, Derek? What the hell do you want?"

Restless movement at her side caught Betsy's attention, and she glanced at the girl, lowering her voice.

"And who's this? Why is she here?"

Derek crooked a finger at the girl, and before Betsy could stop her, she vaulted off the couch and ran to him. He hoisted her on his lap where she laid her head on his shoulder.

"This is Mary. You remember Rico?"

Betsy nodded. Derek's right hand man for years before she'd even come into the picture, Rico had been a calming influence on Derek, though no one really knew why. He was brusque, bad-tempered and was constantly hitting on any female within spitting distance, including Betsy. His death had hit Derek hard.

"Mary is Rico's kid. Her momma asked me to take care of her for awhile. I told her we'd be happy to. Figured our Ainsley would appreciate having someone to play with."

"This isn't..."

Derek held a hand up, then put Mary on the floor. "Why don't you go play in your room for a bit, okay? I'll come get you when we're done talking." After a tentative look at Betsy, she ran off, and Derek paced the center of the room.

"You know what I want," he said, stopping in front of her. "I want what we had - what we should have had. I want my wife, and my daughter, and for all of us to be together. Happily ever after, and all that crap. And that's what I'm going to get, dammit. That's what I deserve."

Betsy stood up, meeting his gaze straight on. "Happily ever after for who, Derek. For you? Because there wasn't anything *happy* about us when you went to jail. There's nothing *happy* about your husband almost killing you. There's nothing *happy* about spending all that time in the hospital, wondering if the jury's going to let your husband go free so he can finish the job. My happily ever after started the day they put you behind bars, and I'll be damned if I'm going to give it up now."

* * *

Ian tugged at the ropes one last time, making sure the goon who'd nearly shot him wasn't going anywhere. He hoped Derek had heard the shot, and assumed he was dead. His only chance at getting Betsy out of there alive was the element of surprise. Ian tucked the other man's gun in the back of his waistband just in case, and then stepped carefully up the back stairs and let himself into the cabin.

Careful not to let the back door slam behind him and staying low, he moved into the hall, thankful for the thin rug that muffled his steps on the hardwood floor. Finally reaching the corner, he crouched and peered into the living room, heart pounding in his chest as he watched Betsy tell her ex that she didn't want his happily ever after. Derek's grip tightened on the gun in his hand, his finger moving to the trigger, and when he started to raise his arm, Ian didn't hesitate.

"Hold it right there," he said, his own gun pointed at Derek's chest as he walked into the room. "I'd suggest you drop that weapon before I make sure you can't ever pick one up again."

Derek laughed, an evil sound that crawled up Ian's spine and threatened to make him shake.

"You don't want to do this, preacher. Someone's gonna get hurt bad, and it ain't gonna be me." Before Ian could guess his intentions, Derek reached out and grabbed Betsy's wrist, pulling her hard so she stumbled against him. Pinned against his chest, Betsy struggled to breathe as he squeezed a thick forearm against her throat.

The gun rested across Betsy's middle, Derek's finger still on the trigger as he fought to subdue the wiggling woman in his grasp. Ian hesitated for a second, though it seemed like an eternity. Betsy's lips were moving, mouthing the words he needed to hear in order to proceed.

Do it.

He raised the gun and pulled the trigger in one smooth motion, his arm never wavering as the shock traveled up to his shoulder and back and the sound echoed in the room. Derek's eyes widened briefly before a perfect round red dot appeared on his forehead, and then he was falling backwards, taking Betsy down with him. They landed on the floor with a thud and Ian ran over, pulling Betsy up off the floor and into his embrace.

She clung to him, burying her face in his chest as he held her and watched the blood pool underneath Derek's head.

"Are you okay?" he asked, gently running his hands over her arms and back. She nodded, swiping at the tears on her face and then glancing over her shoulder at the body on the floor.

"I can't believe you shot him." She stepped back, then her eyes widened before she turned to look toward the staircase. "The little girl - I have to find her. And Ainsley..."

"Go find them. I'll call the police." Ian pulled out the cell phone and dialed 9-1-1, hoping the nightmare was finally over.

* * *

Betsy ran toward the stairs and started up, relieved to see Mary waiting at the top. Tears streamed down the little girl's face as Betsy scooped her up and hugged her tight.

"It's okay, sweetheart. Everything's going to be fine." She pulled her head back so she could look at Mary's face. "Do you know where Ainsley is? Is she here?"

Mary hesitated, then pointed over Betsy's shoulder. Turning, Betsy saw a partially open door on the other side of the cabin. She ran to it, only vaguely aware of Mary's cries growing louder. Setting the girl down in the hall, she nudged the door open with one foot and hoped no one else was in the room. A small figure lying in the center of a bed caught her eye and she dared to hope as she crossed the room in three strides. Relief turned to horror when she saw the bright red stain spreading under the girl, and the blood seeping too fast from a hole in the center of her little chest.

"No no no no no!" Betsy grabbed a blanket from the end of the bed and pressed it to Ainsley's wound, even though she knew it was far too late. Feeling for a pulse, she didn't turn when heavy footsteps approached and strong hands closed over her upper arms, pulling her away.

Sirens grew louder as Ian wrestled her away, his arms reaching out to wrap her little girl in the blanket and scoop her off the bed. Numb, she followed, picking Mary up again as they hurried downstairs and out to the front porch. Laying Ainsley on the hardwood planks he pressed the blanket into her chest with both hands, his lips moving silently as they waited for the ambulance.

It was no use, Betsy knew. She hugged Mary as an ambulance, two sheriff's cars and a work truck with a firefighter insignia on it all pulled up to the house. Paramedics ran out, brushing Ian aside to tend Ainsley, but it wasn't long before she saw one of them check his watch after the other shook her head.

Deputies guided her off the porch, one of them taking Mary from her. Everything was blurry, moving in slow motion as a white sheet was laid over Ainsley's body. She looked around, trying to find Ian, but he seemed to have disappeared. Voices kept asking her what happened, if she was okay, what her name was, but she couldn't seem to find the words. Someone wrapped a blanket around her shoulders. A bottle of water was pressed into her hand. She followed directions, ducking her head when an officer guided her into the back seat of his cruiser.

At the station, she followed obediently to a bright room and took the offered seat at a cold metal table. Two suits came in and sat across from her, exchanging a certain look before one of them spoke.

"Ma'am, we're very sorry and I know it's hard, but we really need you to tell us what happened in that cabin."

Betsy shook her head, tears seeping out onto her cheeks at the truth. She'd told Ian to shoot. It had been her words that killed Ainsley.

"We shot my daughter," she said, her chest squeezing tight as she spoke the words.

The interrogator looked up, eyebrows raised. "The girl..." he glanced down at the papers in front of him, then back up at her. "Ainsley Watters was your daughter?"

Betsy nodded, flicking helplessly at a tear. "Biologically speaking. The Watters adopted her as a baby. I...it was the only way to protect her. I had to make sure she was safe, and now..." She shook her head, taking the tissue offered by the as yet silent detective. "It didn't matter. None of it mattered, in the end."

One of the men cleared his throat, the sound of papers rustling loud in the too-small space. She looked up to find them looking at each other, a silent conversation before they turned back to her. The first man - he'd mentioned his name when they came in, but she couldn't remember it - laid his pen down on the table and leaned back in his chair.

"Maybe you could start from the beginning, ma'am. Who were the men in the cabin, and why were you all there?"

Betsy wiped her nose, breathing a few times to compose herself. The detectives' expressions implied they were expecting an answer, but even in her grief she knew better. She'd been here before, in another life.

"I want my phone call. I'm not saying anything without my lawyer." Harley had better pick up the damn phone. Surely his well-paid team of lawyers would know what to do for her and Ian.

Dark, disapproving scowls gave her a strange sense of satisfaction as the two men gathered their files and walked out the door. She relaxed in her seat, as much as she could, and prepared herself for the inevitable wait. It would be awhile before they either brought her a phone, or took her to one. Trying to block images of Ainsley out of her head, she wondered where Ian was, and what he was doing. She hadn't seen him since the cops had cuffed him back at the cabin, but she knew he'd be blaming himself too.

Again she thought about that moment, the single point in time when she'd lost everything. Replaying it in slow motion, she saw herself giving Ian the okay. The blast as the gun went off, a sharp crack as it entered Derek's forehead, the world off kilter as Derek's muscles contracted around her.

A second shot from somewhere close by as she and Derek hit the floor.

The door opened and she looked up, trying to re-focus on the present. A tall, clean-cut man in an expensive gray suit and a maroon shirt walked in like he owned the place, laying a briefcase on the table.

"Ms. Majors?" he said, waiting for her nod to continue. "I'm Bruce Swenson, your attorney. Your brother sent me." He held out a hand, his grip firm around hers when she shook it. Pulling back, he took a notepad and tape recorder out of the case and sat across from her, perching reading glasses low on his nose. Finding a pen, he rested his forearms on the table and looked at her over the lenses.

"First things first," he said, pushing a button on the recorder. "I need you to tell me exactly what happened at the cabin, starting with when you arrived."

Chapter Thirteen

Betsy shook her head. "First, I'll need to speak with Harley. They haven't given me my phone call yet. And no offense, but I don't recognize you, so I'll need a business card too." She waited patiently, holding the man's unblinking stare with as firm an expression as she could muster. Harley's lawyers were old school - they'd been around the block. This guy looked like he'd just taken the bar, and worse, he reminded her of the kind of suits Derek used to keep around for dubious effect.

Long fingers reached out and turned off the recorder. "Here's my card," he said, pulling one out of his jacket pocket and sliding it across the table to her. "Your brother's a little tied up right now, but if there's someone else you want to call, I can arrange for that."

"Why?" she asked, leaning forward. "What is Harley doing? Tell him I need him, that it's important. He can't take three minutes to talk to his sister?"

Swenson tilted his head thoughtfully. "When was the last time you spoke with Mr. Majors? There's been a lot going on at the ranch - you're telling me you haven't heard about any of it?"

Betsy's stomach flipped over, and a new wave of nausea hit her. "I've been...a little busy myself. What happened? Is he okay?" She looked up at the large one-way mirror, then at the door. "I need to get out of here. Can you make that happen?"

Swenson nodded. "Just tell me what happened, and we should be out of here in no time." He turned the recorder on again and leaned forward, pen poised above a yellow legal pad.

Rubbing her face with her hands, Betsy sighed. Whoever he worked for, he was definitely a lawyer if the card he'd given her was correct, and all that mattered right now was getting out. She sat back and started talking, the whole story tumbling effortlessly from her lips. It was a surreal feeling, laying it all out like that, and she could almost believe that it had happened to someone else. When she got to the end though, she was back in that bedroom, looking down at Ainsley and her heart broke all over again.

"I loved her," she choked out. "I only wanted to keep her safe."

Swenson turned off the tape recorder. "That's enough for today," he said, handing her a tissue. "We'll need to talk more once you're feeling up to it, but this is a good start." He put the recorder and his notes in the briefcase, shutting the clasps with a loud snap that made Betsy twitch.

"I can go home now?" she asked, watching his stoic face closely. "What about Ian?"

The lawyer checked his watch. "Mr. Mitchell should be about done with his interview as well. The detectives will want to speak with you for a minute, but I'll be here the whole time. They don't have any evidence that you were involved in the shooting, so you should be able to leave very soon. Mr. Mitchell is a different story - because he was involved in a shooting, they'll probably want to hold him as long as they can." He picked up his briefcase and went to the door. "I need to step out for a moment and get the detectives."

Betsy nodded, knowing she didn't have any other option. Swenson was back in ten minutes with the same two detectives, who were much more subdued with the lawyer's presence. Twenty minutes later, she was standing in front of the station, watching Swenson drive away.

* * *

Ian let out a long sigh and left the Sheriff's office. His body ached as he strolled into the parking lot under the stark yellow streetlights, and he wondered where Betsy had gone and how he could find her. The detectives had said she was released hours ago, and his heart hurt that he couldn't have been there for her. They'd held him until they could confirm that the bullet that matched Ainsley's wound had come from a gun that matched the caliber of Derek's, clearing him of the murder. Even so, he still felt responsible. He should have waited, should have paid more attention to Derek's position...

"Ian."

He turned, not quite trusting his ears until he saw Betsy's weary face. Haggard and pale, she rose from the bench beside the door. He started to rush forward, but stopped just short of her position. Her expression was unreadable, and he simply held his arms out to either side and waited. He wouldn't blame her if she blamed him. He'd failed to protect the one thing that mattered to her.

He saw the hesitation in her eyes, the questions she needed answers to. He knew he couldn't answer the most important one. She moved closer, holding his gaze, searching his soul. Then she reached up and hooked her arms around his neck, her eyes glittering with unshed tears. Ian folded her into his arms, holding her tight as she finally let the dam burst.

Words came to his lips and died, none of them quite what he wanted to say or, he suspected, what she needed to hear. Empty platitudes is all they would be - just noise to fill up a silence better left alone. He held her while she cried, her tears soaking his neck as he blinked back the moisture in his own eyes. When she quieted, he slowly rubbed her back, rocking her side to side.

"Did you call Harley?" he asked finally, pulling back so he could see her face. Gently moving the hair out of her eyes, he traced the side of her face with his fingers. Something stirred deep inside him when she closed her eyes and leaned into his touch.

"They wouldn't let me - the lawyer he sent said my brother was with the feds or something like that...and when they let me go, my battery was dead." She sniffled, pulling out of his embrace. "I don't know what to do anymore, Ian. How do I tell him about all of this? I never told anyone about Ainsley - not even him. And now she's dead, and it's all my fault..."

She turned away, covering her face with her hands as her shoulders shook with the burden. Ian reached for her, but she pulled away, stumbling forward to lean against a pole. He followed and grasped her arms, turning her into his chest.

"Shh. It's gonna be alright, I promise." He held her again, tears streaking down his own face as her pain became his. "We'll figure it out, and I'll be here, whatever you need."

He wanted to tell her it wasn't her fault, but he knew she wouldn't listen. The best he could do was get her someplace safe where they could rest. Looking out across the lot, he saw a blinking neon hotel sign just across the main road. Rest, a shower and a phone might help put things into perspective.

"Put your arms around my neck, sweetheart," he whispered, guiding her wrists up until he felt her grip just under his hair. Leaning down, he picked her up and snuggled her against his chest as he started walking.

* * *

Betsy tucked her face into Ian's neck as he carried her across the parking lot. It didn't matter where he was taking her. He'd always cared for her, even when they were young, and she knew whatever he had in mind would be exactly what she needed. He had a knack for knowing what to do, and she envied him that. If only she could be that decisive, that confident in her decisions. Maybe life would have turned out differently if she could be more like him.

Maybe Ainsley would still be alive.

She closed her eyes for what felt like a moment until he lowered her into a chair. She blinked her eyes

open, noting the unfamiliar surroundings before looking up at him.

"I'm going to get us a room," he said with a tired
smile. "I'll be right back. Just rest."

Nodding her head, she lay back and let her mind
drift as she waited. Over and over the scene played in
her head - mouthing the words to Ian, the words that
made her responsible for her daughter's death. How
could he still even look at her after what she'd done?
Why was he being so nice? She didn't deserve nice.
She didn't deserve his pity or sympathy or...or him.

She'd never deserved him.

The realization struck at her core and suddenly
everything fell into place. She'd been so blinded by
her hero-worship of him that she'd failed to see it at
first, but she saw it now. All those times he'd gotten
her out of trouble, made sure she got home okay and
listened to her wail about this boy or that...it had all
been because he felt sorry for her, not because he actually had feelings for her. That's why he'd always
pushed her away. She'd been so stupid not to see it
before.

He said he loved her, but had she finally just
worn him down? Did he really care for her, or did he
just feel responsible for her happiness?

Wiping the tears from her face, she got up and
walked to the door, peering out at him standing at the
desk. He'd been so good to her and her heart broke at
the thought of having to leave, but it would be better

this way. For him, at least - and hopefully for her too. Maybe they could both finally find the closure they were looking for.

Moving quietly, she slipped out the side door and away from the building, energy and angst fueling her flight. Running as fast as she could, she reached the next side street and hid behind a house when he ran out of the hotel calling her name. When he finally gave up and went back inside, she jogged in the opposite direction. She'd find a phone, call a cab, and go back to the ranch long enough to get her things and say goodbye to Harley. It was time to make some changes. Time to take care of herself for a change, instead of expecting others to do it for her.

* * *

By the time Betsy walked through the main gate of Fantasy Ranch, she just wanted to crawl into bed and never come out. Her heart hurt, but at the same time it felt empty, her spirit broken.

As she trudged down the dirt roads toward the mansion, she wondered at the quiet. The sun was coming up, and normally the staff would be bustling around from building to building, preparing for the day. It was like a ghost town, but she didn't have the strength to care aside from the passing observation.

Entering the mansion through the back door, she walked through the eerily silent kitchens, her footsteps echoing as she moved down the hall to the grand staircase and called the hidden elevator.

Tired. So tired.

Below, the silence continued. She went to her suite and unlocked the door, locking it behind her and dropping the keys on the side table. Once in the bedroom, she looked at her bed, then at her closet. She should pack. Ian would be looking for her, and he'd come here first. She needed to be gone before he found her.

Indulging in a wide yawn, she went to the closet and pulled out a suitcase, laying it open on the end of her bed. Not bothering to look at what she was grabbing, she tossed random items of clothing into the case until it was full. Then she went to the dresser for underwear and socks, stuffing them into the empty corners and front pockets. Hurt and anger and loss all forced their way to the surface as she worked, much to her dismay. The more she felt, the angrier she got, until she was just randomly throwing things across the room.

She didn't even realize she was crying until the drops fell on her arm, and she looked down in surprise.

Collapsing face down across the bed, she grabbed a pillow and buried her face in it, trying to stifle the tears, and with them the hurt. Images of Ian from years ago, of Ainsley, even Derek in happier times flitted through her mind, and she longed to rewind her life, to undo all the pain of the past few days.

But it wasn't possible.

Exhausted and hopeless, she closed her eyes and drifted off to sleep.

Chapter Fourteen

"Betsy! Are you in there?"

The words barely penetrated the fog in her brain, and she struggled to decide whether she was dreaming or not. Again, someone called out her name, the shout accompanied by a low thumping that seemed to reverberate through her skull. She burrowed further into the pillow, then moved it to cover her head. The world could go away - she wasn't ready to face it again yet.

A loud crash sent a jolt of adrenaline through her body, and she groaned, pushing up off the bed as footsteps thundered toward her room. For a moment, she shrank up against the wall, cringing at the thought of Derek coming to beat her.

The door to her room burst open, and Harley stood there staring at her, his chest heaving at the effort.

Derek is dead, she remembered as she watched her brother walk across the room. He sat on the bed beside her, concern in his normally hard eyes.

"Ian called and wanted to know if you were here. He said you left him at some hotel..." he paused, his brows drawn together. "He said Derek is dead, sis - is that true? And some little girl he said you'd have to tell me about. What's going on, Betsy?"

She shook her head, looking away. "It doesn't matter now, Harley. None of it matters." She scooted past him and got off the bed, rubbing her face with her hands. "I need to leave," she said, going to her suitcase and checking the closures. "I appreciate everything you've done, and I love the ranch, but I need to take care of myself for awhile." She looked into his eyes, holding a hand up when he started to argue. "Do you realize I've never done that? There's always been you, or Derek, and then Ian...I've never actually been on my own before, and I think it's time I found out what that's like."

"Is that really the reason you're leaving?" Harley went to the door, leaning against the frame and effectively blocking her path. "Or is it because you're scared to face everything that's happened in the past few days? And what might happen between you and Ian if you stay."

Betsy shrugged. "That's part of what I need to figure out. But every time I look at him, I think about my daughter, and those last few shots - how I told

him to do it." She looked at her brother, smiling sadly
at his quizzical expression. "I never told you I had a
daughter. I'm sorry." She sat down on the bed, looking at her hands in her lap. "Her name was Ainsley. I
got pregnant right before Derek got sent to jail. He
kidnapped her to get to me, and she was upstairs
when Ian shot Derek. Derek's gun was pointed up..."
She shook her head, knowing it all sounded like a big
accident, but it felt like something much more sinis-
ter.

"She's dead, Harley. I never even got to know her
much, just watched from outside the yard. Maybe if I
hadn't given her up, or if I hadn't lived so close to
her, she'd still be safe. Alive."

A warm hand slid over her shoulder, pulling her
close and she leaned into him, accepting the comfort.
It hurt that she had to leave him - leave everyone behind, but she needed time to think.

Time to heal.

Harley took something out of his pocket, then
knelt down in front of her.

"I understand that you need some time alone," he
said, placing a key in her hand, and then grasping her
fingers in his. "But you have to understand, I can't
just let you go anywhere. I need to know where you
are, and that you're safe. Especially after today."

Betsy looked down at the dull metal object. It was
more of a skeleton key than a modern one, though
there was a distinct pattern cut into one edge.

"What's this go to? I thought we had all the locks updated two years ago."

He smiled. "Remember that little cabin we thought would make a good homestead-style overnight rental at the back of the property? There's not much out there, but it's private, and you'd still be close but you could have all the time you need to think through whatever it is you need to think through."

She thought about it for a moment. "Does Ian know it's there?"

"I do. But I'll leave you alone, if that's what you want."

At the low voice behind him, Harley stepped aside. "I was wondering when you were gonna show up," he said, shaking hands with the minister. Ian looked tired, Betsy noted. Part of her wanted to run to him, to apologize and melt into his arms. He'd tell her it would all be okay, and she'd believe him, because she wanted to.

But it wasn't. It might not ever be. And that's why she needed some space.

She stood up and pulled her suitcase off the bed, slinging her purse over one shoulder. "I'll go out to the cabin, but you both have to promise not to come out there. Not for anything, do you understand? You have to leave me alone, or I'll leave the ranch."

There was a moment of hesitation, a look exchanged between the two men before both finally nodded.

"Agreed," Harley said. "Just...try not to stay away too long, okay?"

She gave him a terse nod, then eased past the them, fighting the urge to look back as she left the suite.

* * *

Ian watched Betsy walk out the door, his heart following her even as he forced his body to remain in place. She was running scared, which wasn't surprising, given her history. What he couldn't figure out was if it was the past or the future that scared her the most.

"You should get some sleep," Harley said, drawing Ian's attention back. "You look like death warmed over. And you know how she gets when she makes up her mind to do something. Nothing you can do now but wait." He clamped a hand on Ian's shoulder, strong and supportive.

Ian nodded. "I know. If she'd just talk to me--"

"She knows that." Harley stepped around to meet Ian's gaze with a hard stare. "Do you love her? I mean, after all this time, everything she's put you through - do you really love her?"

"I do." Ian lowered his head, fighting the discomfort of being so exposed in front of Betsy's brother.

His best friend.

"Well then, you're just going to have to convince her to trust you. But you're both tired, and I guarantee she's not going to talk to you or anyone else until you both get some sleep. So go on, get out of here. You'll know what to do when you wake up."

Ian held out his hand. "Thanks Harley. You know I appreciate it." Taking his hand, Harley pressed something small and cold against Ian's palm before he let go.

"I know," Harley smiled. "I've been rooting for you since day one, way back when we were kids. Don't blow it this time, okay?"

"I'll do my best." Ian chuckled, following Harley into the hall. The key Harley had given him was identical to the one he'd given Betsy, and while he knew he needed to bide his time, Ian was grateful for the gesture.

He walked with Harley to the elevators and let himself out, but instead of heading straight for the chapel, he veered off into the trees. The sun was slipping away, leaving the forest cool and dim as he moved farther away from the main compound. There was a trail, if he recalled correctly, but Betsy would probably be on it, and he didn't want to bother her anymore than he already had. He just wanted to make sure she was safe. Then he'd go back.

By the time he reached the clearing, there was a light on in the single window at the front of the little cabin. Peering out from behind a thick tree, Ian watched as Betsy opened the door and went to the wood pile a few feet away, gathering logs and carrying them back into the small structure. Soon enough, smoke came out of the rock chimney, and he could imagine her sitting by the fire, staring into the flames.

He wished he could be there with her, holding her. He'd spent most of his life telling himself it would never happen, that he wasn't the right man for her - and maybe it was still true. But after being inside her the other night, seeing the look in her eyes, feeling the tension that connected them in a way he'd never felt with anyone else...he couldn't just let her go without a fight.

Turning away, he forced himself to go back to the chapel, the walk feeling far longer than it had before. He let himself into his rooms and locked the doors, glancing at the walls as if he'd never seen them before. The whole building was decorated for a proper minister, a man of God who lived a pure life. It was all for show, of course - he'd never attended a seminary, and he wasn't even particularly religious, though he did believe in some sort of higher power. But the ranch was built on fantasy, and he was part of that. Given his introverted nature and quiet personality, it was easy to see why Betsy had fallen for his fictional persona.

The question was, did she want the man, or the fantasy? Over the past few days, she'd gotten to know the man, instead of the character he'd used for so many years to keep a wall between them. Maybe the man just wasn't enough.

* * *

"You might as well come out," Betsy called, rubbing her hands together in the cool evening air. "You never were very good at hide and seek."

It had been a week, and though she hated to admit it, she was tired of her own company. She'd cried, yelled, and spent a lot of time just reflecting on her life - wondering how it had gotten so far off track. It was obvious, of course, once she stopped to really think about it, but as hard as she tried she couldn't say she would have done anything differently. Her decisions had all come down to where she was at that point in her life, and choosing any other path just...wouldn't have been her.

As she watched Ian emerge from a thicket of brambles, trying in vain to brush off the stickers, she knew that all she could do now is what she'd always done. In order to move forward, she had to make decisions based on who she was now, nothing else. It was the only way to be true to herself.

"I was...um...just out for a walk," Ian started, abandoning the lie when she shook her head. His lips curved up in a half-grin as he came closer, stopping just out of reach.

"You've been watching me all week." Betsy noted his surprise with satisfaction. "You break twigs, you crunch leaves, and you really don't blend in with the scenery. But thank you for at least respecting my space enough to keep your distance."

He nodded, dropping his gaze to the ground as he scuffed the toe of one hiking boot in the dirt.

"I just wanted to make sure you were okay," he said, that rich, low voice doing lovely things to her insides. "I wanted to be close. In case you needed me."

When he looked up, she nearly melted at the sincerity and concern in those gorgeous eyes of his. She searched for the expected pity or obligation, but there was none. She'd kept telling herself that the concerns the night she ran off were unfounded, and that she'd overreacted out of fear of how strong her feelings for him were. But to be able to see how much he cared as he took a step closer to the small porch made it that much easier to believe.

"I told you if you didn't stay away, I'd leave the ranch."

His eyes narrowed, ever so slightly. "Like you said, I've been around all week. So why are you still here?"

Betsy shrugged, looking down at her hands. "I'm not sure, exactly." She turned, pacing the small wooden decking. "A week ago, I would have said fear.

Two days ago, I might have said laziness. And today..." The board behind her creaked, and she turned to find Ian standing there, his broad chest enticing her to lean in just a little more.

"Today?" he repeated softly, his hands reaching out to caress her arms. It took every bit of strength she had to refrain from touching him back.

"Choices," she murmured, looking up at him and making the choice she wished she'd been strong enough to make years ago. "Today is about choices."

Betsy reached for Ian, burying her fingers in the front of his shirt as she went up on tiptoe to press her lips to his. His arms slid around her back as he pulled her up tight against his body, practically devouring her mouth as he took control of the kiss. Her body throbbed in welcome desire, and she eagerly gave him as much as he would take, overwhelmed by the sheer power enveloping her.

His pelvis rocked against hers, the hard bulge unmistakable as he showed her what he wanted. The ache between her legs grew stronger, and her nipples begged for release as they pressed into the hard muscles of his torso.

"Too many clothes, Bets..." he murmured against her lips just before he pulled away and spun her toward the door. "I need you naked. Now."

She giggled. "Now Ian, is that any way for a preacher to talk?" She darted inside the cabin and ran for the bedroom, hearing his footsteps as he followed close behind. She slowed as she approached the small bed, turning just in time to see his grin as he tackled her down to the quilt. Taking her hand, he pressed it against his groin and she curled her fingers around his thick cock, teasing him through his jeans.

"God wouldn't have given me this if he didn't want me to use it, darlin'. I don't intend to let it get dusty with you around."

She found his zipper and pulled it down, the low groan he let out going straight to her core. "You've got nothing to worry about there, mister. I'm a very good maid, though I can't say I take orders very well." She reached up and pushed hard at his shoulder, knocking him to his back and then straddling his thighs. A flick of her hands opened the button on his jeans and she retrieved his cock, slowly stroking him up and down in her palm. His eyes closed and his head fell back as she moved back and then bent to run her tongue over the tip of his rod.

"Honey, you can do whatever you want as long as you keep touching me."

She swirled around and over, tracing the hard lines and veins as his legs moved restlessly beneath her. One hard thigh pushed between her knees to press against her center, and she nearly came right then from the pressure as she sucked him deep into her mouth.

Ian's hands framed her face, gently tugging her up for a kiss as she sprawled on top of his body. Rolling her under him, he kissed her chin, her jaw, her neck, and then down the front of her chest as he undid each button, one by one. Bracing himself on his elbows, he spread her shirt with one hand, kissing each breast where it peeked over her bra before he opened the center clasp and freed her to his view.

"Beautiful," he whispered, laving one nipple, then the other with his tongue. Moving back and forth, he suckled and nipped and lavished attention until she couldn't have formed a coherent thought to save her life. When he moved lower, placing soft, moist kisses along her ribcage, her stomach, and coaxing her pants past her hips and down her legs, she wasn't sure she could handle much more. It was...he was too much, and at the same time, she needed more.

"Please," she breathed, moving restlessly as he discarded his clothes. "I need--"

"I know, baby." He licked and nipped his way up the inside of her thigh, then repeated the process on her other leg, finishing with one smooth stroke over her full, inner lips. Betsy bucked up off the bed and he covered her mound with his lips, his tongue teasing and probing at her clit. She was already so close...

The intensity of the tremors surprised her when they hit just a few seconds later. Radiating out from where Ian's skillful mouth was still busy, the quick pulses spread throughout her body light lightening, leaving complete bliss in their wake.

"Ian?" She couldn't remember the last time she'd felt so good, so relaxed. The man responsible moved up her body, his fingers sliding up her skin inch by glorious inch until he covered her with his hard warmth.

"Yes Betsy?" His cock probed at her entrance, teasing as she looked up into his eyes. The emotions she saw there mirrored her own, giving her the courage for what she needed to say. She raised a hand to his chiseled face and smiled.

"I love you, Ian. I'm sorry it took me so long to realize it, but I do."

He slid home smooth and easy, then leaned down for a kiss. "I love you too. Always have, always will." Holding her gaze, he set a slow rhythm with his hips that stoked the fire with every thrust. His gaze was mesmerizing, and she couldn't look away as he brought her higher with him. The heat between them built to a fever pitch, and just when she thought she couldn't take anymore it exploded into an indescribable array of light.

Chapter Fifteen

Betsy focused on breathing as she slowly came back to earth. Ian rolled to the side and she wanted to protest, but didn't have the strength. Still, when he pulled her toward him and tucked her next to his side with her head on his chest, she was relieved that it wasn't all a dream.

The haze lifted, and reluctantly she acknowledged that one of them would eventually have to say something. She ran her fingers over Ian's chest, tracing slow patterns over and around his muscles as she searched for the right words. There were none, though. Everything she could possibly think of was just stupid or cheesy, even in her own mind. The silence stretched on, past the point of comfort, and her insecurities started crowding out her better judgment.

Why hadn't he said anything? Was he trying to figure out how to let her down easy? Had he only said he loved her in the heat of passion, and now regretted it? There was a tiny little voice telling her she was being an idiot, but the other voices were louder. What if he thought she was having second thoughts? Shouldn't she say...something? But why did she have to be first?

No. She loved him. And he loved her, and she wasn't going to accept anything less. Not this time. Not with Ian.

Pushing up on one elbow, so she could look at him when she set him straight about how they felt, she froze when he smiled up at her. His eyes spoke volumes, and suddenly all her panic drained away.

"Marry me, Betsy."

It wasn't really a question, nor was it a command. It was more like a statement of fact. Their destiny.

She didn't mind at all.

"Of course I will."

He reached up and pulled her head down for a kiss, his lips moving slow and gentle against hers as she snuggled close.

Right where she belonged.

* * *

Six months later...

"You may kiss the bride."

Ian raised the gauzy veil from Betsy's face, only vaguely aware of the cheers and shouts from the crowd behind them. Bending down, he cupped her cheek in his hand and placed a long, slow kiss on her carefully colored lips. Her arms slid around his neck, and he pulled her tight to his chest as her tongue mated with his. The din grew louder, and reluctantly he pulled back.

"What do you say we skip the reception and just go straight to the honeymoon?" he whispered, earning a giggle and a slap on the arm. Seeing her so happy, the lines of worry erased from around her eyes made his heart swell with love. He still couldn't believe this gorgeous, outgoing creature was his now. It was both exhilarating and scary.

"Not a chance, stud," she said, pulling him down the stairs. "These people came to celebrate with us, and we aren't going to let them down." She leaned in closer. "Don't you worry, Ian. I promised to take good care of you, and I will. Later."

He rolled his eyes, earning another laugh before they took their place in the receiving line and began to greet their guests as people filed out of the castle's great hall. It took forever, it seemed, but finally they were free to join everyone in the courtyard for a modified medieval feast. They'd decided not to go as far as costumes, but the castle wedding seemed like a perfect compromise between formality and a casual feel. Or that's what Betsy and the other women had said.

Ian had stayed out of most of the plans, content to let Betsy run the show. As long as they were married in the end, he hadn't been too concerned with how it happened.

Ian didn't care. He stood off to the side sipping hard cider out of a silver goblet as he watched his bride happily flit from table to table. They'd already started learning to live with each others differences - she was so outgoing, and seemed to feed off interacting with others, while he found it exhausting, and needed time to himself. But somehow, it worked, and she waved at him from across the courtyard as he smiled and raised his glass in return.

"Excuse me, sir? Do you know where I might find Monica...um...Majors?"

Ian looked down to find a petite woman at his side, her hair pulled back in a simple clasp and her features unmistakable, even with the extra lines of age.

He smiled, offering his arm. "You must be her mother. I'm really glad you could make it - I know she's looking forward to seeing you." Monica had been sold as a child, her mother blackmailed to give her up. She'd only found out several months ago when her father tried to take over the ranch from Harley for daring to help Monica escape his plans for her. It had been a rough road, and she deserved some peace about her past.

The woman nodded, her hand trembling as she placed it on his arm. "Brenda Davis," she said, her lips curving up only slightly. "I wasn't sure I should come, but I just couldn't stay away any longer."

Ian led her toward the quiet table in the corner where Harley and Monica were sitting alone. "Monica," he said, the grip on his arm tightening ever so slightly when his new sister-in-law looked up at them. "I'd like to introduce Brenda Davis. Your mother."

Monica rose from her seat to come forward, and her mother's hand slipped from his arm. The women stared at each other for a long moment, and then they were in each others arms.

Harley nodded at Ian, and Ian raised his glass once more before turning back to the crowd. Monica would want some time alone with Brenda, and he was about ready to toss Betsy over his shoulder and carry her off to his rooms, caveman style if necessary.

Tossing back the rest of his drink, he started across the large expanse of lawn and wooden tables. Just his luck, Betsy was all the way across the courtyard and every time Ian took a few more steps, someone had to stop and congratulate him again. He smiled and nodded and shook hands like he was supposed to, keeping his eye on the prize, and reminding himself that she was the reason he was doing this.

It was worth every second.

"Excuse me, sir."

He looked down at a tug on the sleeve of his jacket. A petite brunette blinked up at him, shading her eyes from the sun with one hand. He didn't recognize her, but he didn't recognize half the people here. She looked frustrated.

"What can I do for you?" he asked, trying to decide how old she was. Though small of stature, the lines on her face suggested she was well out of college. An odd dichotomy.

She scanned the crowd, then looked back up at him. "I can't find my date. I was wondering if you'd help me? He's over six feet, with brown hair that curls at his shoulders and he's wearing a black suit and white shirt with no tie. You'd think I'd be able to see him at his height, but there are so many of you tall men here..."

Ian chuckled, wisely refraining from a response, considering she was shorter than most women in attendance. She couldn't be more than five feet tall, if that. And she was wearing heels, he noted.

He turned a circle as he searched the crowd, but the only man who fit that description was the handyman, Chance Emery. Ian could have sworn he came in with Veronica Rowan, though she didn't seem to be around at the moment.

He pointed that direction. "Chance is the only guy without a tie here, I think, but he's with--"

The woman smiled, holding up a hand. "That's him. I'd better get over there before he leaves me.

Thank you!" She hurried off before Ian could say another word. He thought about sticking around to watch the fireworks - Veronica didn't seem to be the type who would share, but then Betsy called his name and he remembered his mission.

Knowing it was rude, he pretended not to hear his own name as he strode to where she was waiting.

"I was watching you," she said as he pulled her into his arms. "I thought you'd never get here."

He grinned, placing a light kiss on her lips that raised another chorus of catcalls and hollering behind them. "Me either. I think I deserve a reward, don't you?"

She smiled up at him. "What did you have in mind?"

He wiggled his eyebrows, kissed the tip of her nose, and then bent down to grab her around the waist, lifting her up over his shoulder and holding her dress down around her legs.

Caveman style.

"Ian, what are you doing? Let me down! What about the cake? And the band?!"

The crowd went wild with laughter and lewd comments as Ian headed for the exit. "We can do cake later," he said, low enough so only she could hear. "Right now, there's only one thing I'm interested in 'doing', and that's you, Mrs. Mitchell. Wave goodbye to your friends."

He carried her out the gate, a little worried that she was so quiet. Once they were away from the castle though, he felt her hands caressing his back.

"Ian? Darling?"

"Yes love?"

"If you put me down, we can get home faster..."

About the Author

A full-time webmistress by day, Jamie DeBree writes steamy, action-packed romantic suspense late into the night. Her goal is to create the perfect blend of sensual attraction, emotional tension and fast-paced adventure, similar to the television crime dramas she's hopelessly addicted to.

Born in Billings Montana, she resides there with her husband and two over-sized lap dogs. She reads in a wide variety of genres including romance, erotica, action/adventure, thriller, horror and literary.

For information on upcoming books, visit jamiedebree.com.

www.ingramcontent.com/pod-product-compliance
Lightning Source LLC
Chambersburg PA
CBHW051824170626
46807CB00003B/1021